"You seem nervous around me."

Even as Pete spoke those words, he advanced on her, his eyes never leaving hers.

"I am," Thomasina replied. "We don't fit together, Pete. I'm a career woman. You're an old-fashioned guy. It'd be a mistake for us to get too close."

Close was exactly what they were now. He stood mere inches from her as he said, "It felt pretty good the other day when I held you."

"Use your head, Pete. This'll never work."

He took her by the shoulders, closing the tiny gap between them. "It's not my head I want to use. It's my lips." A millisecond later his mouth claimed hers and his arms wrapped around her.

Any protest she could muster disappeared like mist, and her heart raced. But how could that be? Pete Schofield was not *The One*.

Or was he?

Dear Reader,

Working with talented writers is one of the most rewarding aspects of my job. And I'm especially pleased with this month's lineup because these four authors capture the essence of Silhouette Romance. In their skillful hands, you'll literally feel as if you're riding a roller coaster as you experience all the trials and tribulations of true love.

Start off your adventure with Judy Christenberry's *The Texan's Reluctant Bride* (#1778). Part of the author's new LONE STAR BRIDES miniseries, a career woman discovers what she's been missing when Mr. Wrong starts looking an awful lot like Mr. Right. Patricia Thayer continues her LOVE AT THE GOODTIME CAFÉ with *Familiar Adversaries* (#1779). In this reunion romance, the hero and heroine come from feuding families, but they're about to find out there really is just a thin line separating hate from love! Stop by the BLOSSOM COUNTY FAIR this month for Teresa Carpenter's *Flirting with Fireworks* (#1780). Just don't get burned by the sparks that fly when a fortune-teller's love transforms a single dad. Finally, Shirley Jump rounds out the month with *The Marine's Kiss* (#1781). When a marine wounded in Afghanistan returns home, he winds up helping a schoolteacher restore order to her classroom…but finds her wreaking havoc to his heart!

And be sure to watch for more great romances next month when Judy Christenberry and Susan Meier continue their miniseries.

Happy reading,

Ann Leslie Tuttle
Associate Senior Editor

Please address questions and book requests to:
Silhouette Reader Service
U.S.: 3010 Walden Ave., P.O. Box 1325, Buffalo, NY 14269
Canadian: P.O. Box 609, Fort Erie, Ont. L2A 5X3

JUDY Christenberry

The Texan's Reluctant *Bride*

Lone Star *Brides*

SILHOUETTE **Romance** ®

Published by Silhouette Books

America's Publisher of Contemporary Romance

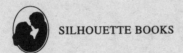 **SILHOUETTE BOOKS**

ISBN 0-373-19778-0

THE TEXAN'S RELUCTANT BRIDE

Visit Silhouette Books at www.eHarlequin.com

Printed in U.S.A.

Books by Judy Christenberry

Silhouette Romance

The Nine-Month Bride #1324
*Marry Me, Kate #1344
*Baby in Her Arms #1350
*A Ring for Cinderella #1356
†Never Let You Go #1453
†The Borrowed Groom #1457
†Cherish the Boss #1463
**Snowbound Sweetheart #1476
Newborn Daddy #1511
When the Lights Went Out… #1547
**Least Likely To Wed #1570
Daddy on the Doorstep #1654
**Beauty & the Beastly Rancher #1678
**The Last Crawford Bachelor #1715
Finding a Family #1762
††The Texan's Reluctant Bride #1778

*The Lucky Charm Sisters
†The Circle K Sisters
**From the Circle K
††Lone Star Brides

Silhouette Books
Hush

The Coltons
The Doctor Delivers

A Colton Family Christmas
"The Diplomat's Daughter"

Lone Star Country Club
The Last Bachelor

JUDY CHRISTENBERRY

has been writing romances for over fifteen years because she loves happy endings as much as her readers do. She's a bestselling author for Harlequin American Romance, but she has a long love of traditional romances and is delighted to tell a story that brings those elements to the reader. A former high school French teacher, Judy devotes her time to writing. She hopes readers have as much fun reading her stories as she does writing them. She spends her spare time reading, watching her favorite sports teams and keeping track of her two adult daughters.

Chapter One

Thomasina Tyler pasted her most charming smile on her face, smoothed down the jacket of her best suit and opened the door to her boss's office.

"Ah, Tommie, come in," Isabel Landon said. "I've been telling Mr. Schofield all about you."

Tommie turned to the gentleman who had risen to his feet as she entered the office, her hand extended. But when she got her first look at the president of the prestigious Boston software company that was moving to Fort Worth, she almost fell off her three-inch heels.

"How do you do, Mr. Schofield," she managed to eke out, hiding her surprise. Peter Schofield was handsome and young and tall. Even wearing heels, she came up only to his mouth. To his perfectly formed lips. He wore a navy suit that was fitted to him like a second skin, no doubt hand-tailored to accentuate his broad shoulders and lean hips. The taupe shirt brought out the gold in his hazel eyes, and his dark hair was short and styled, probably at the best salon in New England. When he smiled at her and his eyes glittered, she almost forgot why she was there. Almost.

Isabel helped bring her to her senses. "Tommie is one of the best Realtors in Fort Worth. I'm sure she'll be able to find you the ideal area for your relocation as well as the perfect houses for you and all your executives."

Tommie's smile widened even more as she considered the future working with this incredible male specimen. "Please come with me to my office and we'll get started on your relocation at once," she said, gesturing to the door.

"With pleasure…" He hesitated, then asked, "May I call you Tommie?"

"Of course."

Isabel had warned her about the upcoming interview and Tommie had thoroughly prepared for it. Too bad her boss hadn't warned her about the man himself, she thought. Nevertheless, in her office she had several areas of town picked out with the advantages of each listed for him to consider. Of course, since Mr. Schofield had grown up in Fort Worth, he might already be familiar with the demographics.

Tommie took another quick look over her shoulder at the transplanted Texan. Forget the beef, the beer, the country music, even the presidents—Peter Schofield was the best thing Texas had ever exported!

Smoothing out her red power suit, she reined in her errant thoughts and reached out to open her office door. Her client beat her to it, holding it open for her to precede him.

"Mrs. Landon assures me you're quite experienced…but you look about eighteen years old," he said on a short but pleasant-sounding laugh.

Tommie was surprised by her lack of indignation. "Let me put your mind to rest, Mr. Schofield. I've been doing this for five years and I've won numerous sales awards." She gestured to the plaques adorning the walls of her office, which was smaller but no less neat and nicely appointed as Isabel's. "And for the record, I'm twenty-six." She sat down behind her desk and pulled out some papers. "The same is true on my part. I expected a grizzled older man who'd fought his battles for years to own his own company. You scarcely have a wrinkle."

He grinned. "I enjoy my work."

He volunteered no vital statistics, though Tommie suspected he couldn't be beyond his early thirties. She immediately got down to business. "On this map of Fort Worth I've targeted three areas that I think you might like. The blue area is located near Texas Christian University. It has a mixture of old and new housing. It's centrally located and has good schools and shopping. The yellow area—" She looked up to find Mr. Schofield staring at her, not the map.

"Is something wrong?"

"No, not at all. Why would you ask that?"

"You weren't looking at the map." In fact, his eyes continued to peer into her own, making her extremely uncomfortable.

"Oh, I was just distracted," he said matter-of-factly. "By your beautiful voice." He cleared his throat and continued without skipping a beat, though her heart had suddenly decided to skip a few. "I'm familiar with Fort Worth. I was born and raised here. Area C is my choice."

"I knew you grew up here, but I wasn't sure you'd selected a particular location yet."

"Yes, I should have told Isabel, but I wasn't positive until I got back home." He looked at her, an apologetic expression on his face.

"I guess I don't have to tell you the advantages of the area, then."

He shook his head, then reached into his breast pocket and withdrew a sheaf of papers. "These are the wish lists from the executives who are making the move. I'm afraid they know nothing of Fort Worth, but I thought the information would help you find houses to fit their needs."

"Thank you so much. You're making my job much easier."

"And more efficient, I hope."

"So I'm assuming time is of the essence?"

He nodded, and the friendly client instantly transformed to a diligent boss. "The sooner we all get settled, the sooner we'll be back at work."

"Very well. Would you like to start looking for your own house first? Or shall I line up houses for your staff?"

"Let's start with me. The others won't be flying in until next week. I'd like to be settled by then."

Tommie thought he was being overly optimistic, but she wasn't going to say anything to discourage him. "I understand. Shall we meet at, say, ten o'clock tomorrow morning? I'll have a list of homes for you to see then."

"Let's meet at nine and I'll buy you breakfast," he countered.

"Fine. Tell me your hotel and I'll pick you up there."

"I'm not staying in a hotel. My mother insisted I stay with her. Here's the address." He leaned in and adopted a conspiratorial tone. "I love the woman, but I can assure you I'm highly motivated to get a place of my own."

Tommie's lips trembled with laughter. She understood exactly what he meant.

Pete found himself smiling the rest of the day as he thought about his Realtor. When Isabel Landon had told him his company move would be handled by Tommie Tyler, Pete had pictured a smarmy salesman and had worried about how he and his executives would work with the man.

Then the door had opened and Tommie Tyler had entered. He figured he'd be seeing the woman in his dreams. She was a beauty. And she'd done her homework. He'd looked at the areas she'd chosen, knowing any of the three would've been fine. He'd chosen the third because his mother and brother lived nearby.

He'd been planning to return to Texas a few years down the road, but he'd pushed up his schedule because of his mother's health. After all, it wasn't fair to leave his brother with all the responsibility.

But there was always a bright side. And he'd met her today. Suddenly, the idea of house hunting would be fun. With Tommie.

When he reached his mother's rambling house, in the most upscale neighborhood in Fort Worth, his brother's car was in the driveway. Pete felt his day was looking up even more. He'd missed Jim. They were twins, and though not identical, they shared the closeness associated with twins.

Jim had stayed at home and attended Texas Christian University, while Pete had gone away to Harvard, and he'd remained in Boston to start his business. Though over a thousand miles apart, they spoke several times a week and Pete knew every detail of his twin's rise to partner at a small local CPA firm.

Their demanding schedules didn't allow for much free time, but they did manage to fit in time for each other and for their mother. Last year she and Jim had visited him in Boston, and they'd recently sent their mother and her friend on the Alaska cruise she'd always spoken of. Pete considered them fortunate to afford such luxuries.

Ms. Tommie Tyler looked as if she appreciated the good things in life herself, judging by her expensive clothes, manicure and coiffed hair. But she'd also demonstrated the priceless things that made life worthwhile. A sense of humor, an active mind and delightful manners.

Pete hoped to delve even further into her personality in the coming days. So far, he'd found nothing to dislike.

He opened the front door to his mother's house.

"Anyone home?" he called.

"Hey, bro, I heard you were back in town," Jim said with a grin as he embraced his brother. He'd worked late the night before and hadn't gotten to see Pete when he'd arrived.

"I'm back to stay this time. How's everything going?"

"According to Mom, everything's coming up daisies since her favorite is back home." Jim rolled his eyes in feigned annoyance.

Pete laughed. "Don't worry. Now that I'm back, I'll soon share the guilt for all the wrongs of the world."

"Damn, I hope so. The burden has been so heavy," Jim teased, joining his brother in laughter.

Arm in arm, they walked into the family room where their mother sat in an oversize upholstered club chair by the window. She was focused, as always, on her knitting. Luckily for the brothers, she no longer made them things; instead, she sent her handmade articles to shelters for the needy.

Evelyn Schofield looked up. Her hair was now more gray than brown and she'd put on a few pounds, but her eyes were as sharp as ever. "Well, I am honored. My two boys here at once. How did the meeting go with Isabel, Pete?"

"Better than I expected, Mom," Pete said with a big smile. "She turned me over to Tommie."

"You're excited about being turned over to Tommie?" Jim asked, frowning.

"You haven't met Tommie. Twenty-six, blond hair, big blue eyes, gorgeous. And I'm taking *her* to breakfast tomorrow morning."

"Hey, can I come along?" Jim asked eagerly, apparently having caught on to the fact that the Realtor was a woman.

"Not on your life! Find your own girl."

"Damn, it's good to have you back," Jim said, hugging Pete again.

"Yes, it is, isn't it," his mother said, smiling at her boys. "Now, who is this Tommie?"

"Her last name is Tyler, but that's all I know. So far."

"Oh," his mother said, suddenly turning her attention to her knitting once again.

"You know her?" Pete asked.

"Why, no, dear, I don't." She got to her feet. "I'm

going to start dinner. Jim has agreed to suffer my cooking this evening, so just make yourselves comfortable."

Jim stared after his mother.

"What?" Pete asked, knowing his brother would understand the question.

"Why would Mom lie about knowing Tommie Tyler?"

"Did she?" Pete asked.

"You've been gone too long, brother. She definitely knows something about the lady. Maybe she knows her mother."

Suddenly a horrific thought struck Pete. "You don't think…" He groaned. "This is all I need, Mom matchmaking. And I'm not even back twenty-four hours."

"Why do you think she's setting you up?"

"Think about it, Jim. She's the one who sent me to Isabel Landon."

"Oh."

"Exactly." He nodded. "Has she been trying to matchmake for you?"

Jim shrugged his shoulders. "I do seem to run into a lot of women…who coincidentally know Mom."

"And you didn't warn me?" Pete asked.

"Are you kidding? I wasn't going to say anything that might make you change your mind about coming home." Jim gave his brother a level look.

"Nothing was going to stop me from coming home now. I should've done it several years ago. But if the medicine I have to take is spending time with Tommie Tyler, I'll just have to suffer through it."

* * *

The Triple T's, as the Tyler triplets called themselves, met for dinner at Teresa's place. She'd promised to cook since school was out and she had plenty of free time.

Though the triplets were mirror images of each other, all with blond hair and big blue eyes, their interests were different, as well as their sense of style.

"So how was everyone's day?" she asked as the three of them sat down at the table.

"Great!" Tabitha said with enthusiasm. She was such a high-energy person that it even filtered into her voice, which was high-pitched and peppy. "I've just about finished working out the first routine for the video. It's going to be great."

Tabitha was in the process of making an exercise and fitness video for teens. "You're definitely going ahead with it?" Tommie asked.

"Yes. I've gotten letters from fifteen school districts interested in seeing the video when I'm finished. I think it's going to do really well."

"That's great, Tabitha," Teresa said, an encouraging smile on her face.

"It is," Tommie agreed, "as long as you're prepared for the opposite happening, too. You won't be hurt if some of them turn you down?"

"No, Tommie, I won't. I've been teaching these kids for four years. Do you think I convince every one of them to keep up an exercise program?" Tabitha asked with a sigh.

"She's just being the big sister, as always," Teresa said.

"Yeah," Tabitha agreed. "She gets a lot of mileage out of those two minutes."

Tommie came to her own defense. "I just worry that you might be disappointed."

"Where were you when Roger dumped me?"

Tommie put her arms around her sister. "Sweetie, I told you he was no good."

Tabitha rolled her eyes. "I know, I know."

Teresa joined the hug. "But you survived, and you always will. After all, you have us," Teresa reminded her. "Come on, eat your dinner before it gets cold. It's a new recipe."

Tommie took a bite and praised her youngest sister's cooking. "This chicken is the best, Teresa. You're such a good cook."

"Thank you," Teresa said with a mock bow. "You haven't said how your day went," she reminded Tommie.

"I think I met The One."

That simple remark got her sisters' attention.

"Who?" Tabitha demanded at the same time as Teresa asked, "Really?"

"Yes, I think so. He's…oh, he's wonderfully handsome."

"But that's not what's important," Teresa reminded her sister.

Tommie lifted her chin and added, "He's also bright, ambitious and kind."

"Who is he?" Tabitha asked.

"Do you remember I told you Isabel was giving me this corporation move? Well, he's the president."

"How old is he?" Teresa asked, looking worried.

"He didn't say, but he didn't look much older than thirty. He's taking me to breakfast in the morning."

"But isn't that the company from Boston? I don't think you should marry a Yankee," Tabitha said.

"Roger was from Texas, wasn't he? Geographic locations don't mean that much. Besides, Pete was born and raised here. And his mother and brother still live here."

"Ah! He has a brother. Only one?" Tabitha asked.

"That's all he mentioned, and he didn't tell me his brother's age, either."

"Tell us about him," Teresa urged.

Tommie put down her fork, a dreamy look on her face. "He's tall, and he has laughing hazel eyes. He's a take-charge kind of guy, but not rigid."

"How much time did you spend with him?" Teresa asked.

"Five minutes."

"And you got all of that in five minutes?" Tabitha asked.

"I'm a good judge of character," Tommie assured her sister. "Remember Roger?"

"I'm sick and tired of hearing about Roger. He's long gone and I'm not crying any tears."

"Not now," Tommie said with sarcasm, because hers had been the shoulder her sister had cried on.

"Just make sure you're not crying over this new guy!" Tabitha retorted.

"Not going to happen. I'm not about to let some guy ruin my life. I've got plans."

"Oh, dear," Teresa muttered.

"What do you mean by that?" Tommie instantly demanded.

"I think she's saying, 'Pride goeth before a fall,'" Tabitha said calmly.

"No, I—" Teresa began, but Tommie didn't let her finish.

"I'm not proud. Just self-assured."

"Did anyone talk to Mom today?" Teresa asked, desperately trying to change the subject.

"I did," Tabitha said. "She said she was a little upset because she'd expected you to come see her since school was out."

"What about you, Tab? School was out for you, too," Tommie pointed out.

"Yes, but I was busy making my video. She understood that. She thinks I'm going to be wildly successful." Tabitha lifted her chin in a challenge to her big sister.

"I don't doubt it, Tabitha," Tommie said gently.

"Me neither," added the other triplet.

Tears pooled in Tabitha's blue eyes, the same blue as her sisters' eyes. She reached for their hands. "You two are the best sisters in the world."

Tommie picked up Pete Schofield at nine o'clock, as he'd requested, and they drove to La Madeleine, a French bakery that served breakfast.

"I wouldn't have picked you for a French-bakery type," Tommie told him after they got their food and were seated.

He grinned. "It's hard to find something that wouldn't be improved with a croissant."

"That's true."

"So, do you know my mother?"

Tommie sat back in her chair, surprise on her face. "What? How would I know your mother?"

"She's lived in Fort Worth all her life. I just thought you might know her."

"Sorry. I didn't grow up in this part of town." It was too upscale from what she'd had as a child. "You may not have noticed, but Fort Worth is a big city now."

Pete watched her, but she showed no signs of lying. He changed the subject. "How did you get started in real estate?"

Tommie shrugged her shoulders. "My mother insisted I get a teaching certificate so I'd always have a job, but it didn't take long after I graduated to figure out that teaching wasn't for me."

"Why?"

"I was trying to teach English to thirty students at a time, five times a day. They didn't want to be there and they let me know it."

"It doesn't sound like enjoyable work."

"It wasn't. But since I loved houses, I decided to try selling them. I got my license at night and found a job with Isabel's company as soon as school was out. And I've been there ever since."

"Have you lined up some places for me to look at today?"

"Yes, I have. I made the assumption that you would prefer a condominium rather than a house since you aren't married and don't have children. There are some very—"

"You're wrong," he said calmly.

"You *are* married?" Tommie asked, her eyes wide. She attributed the sudden pain in her stomach to indigestion, not regret.

"No, I'm not married yet, but I hope to be soon. I want a large family, a house where we can entertain. No condos for me. I had one in Boston, and while it was beautiful, I'm tired of being boxed in."

"Oh, I'm sorry. I should've had you fill out some information for me. But I can line up some houses in this area that might work for you, if you'll give me a few minutes."

"Of course. Finish your breakfast first. I didn't mean you had to work through your meal."

"I don't mind." After she chewed her buttery croissant, she asked, "Does your brother live with your mother?"

Pete grinned. "No. She'd drive him crazy in no time. It's been hard enough for him to be the only son around to torment."

"Torment?"

"Mom can be demanding sometimes."

"So I take it you don't want a house near your mother's?"

"Reasonably close would be okay, but not next door."

"All right, I think I've got the picture. But won't your future wife want to join us?"

Shrugging his shoulders, Pete explained, "I haven't chosen my future wife yet. That's still on my to-do list. But I want a house that will be suitable for the future. I don't plan on moving again anytime soon."

"I see. Is your brother married?"

"Nope. Not yet. He wanted to come meet you today, but I wouldn't let him."

"Why not?"

"We needed to get down to business."

"Yes, well, I'll make a few calls." Tommie pulled out the notebook that showed all the latest listings. She'd gone through all the available houses in the area in preparation for the executives who would be moving with his company.

She wrote down the addresses of the houses she thought he'd be interested in, family houses. She had to call two of the owners to set up appointments. The other two homes she thought would do were standing vacant. They'd go look at those first.

"All right, I'm ready if you are, Mr. Schofield," she said with a bright smile, trying to hide her disappointment at misreading her client's needs.

"Make it Pete."

"All right, Pete. Shall we go?"

"Sure."

After the first house she knew she wasn't hitting the target. "What did you not like about this house?"

"It's not very attractive on the outside. And it needs some work before I could move in."

"I see. Well, I'm not sure about the next one, but we might as well look at it to be sure. The two homes in the afternoon will be more what you're wanting, I think."

"Is there any reason you've lost your enthusiasm?" Pete asked with a frown after they left the next house.

"No. I'm just flustered that I had the wrong kind of homes lined up for you. And I don't feel I'm finding what you want."

"Not yet, but you've only shown me two houses. We'll find something. Let's have lunch."

It bothered Tommie that they were spending more time eating than looking at houses. She might be disappointed that he was hoping to be a family man, with wife and children in his future plans. It made her revise her feelings toward Pete. But that didn't mean she couldn't sell a house to him.

As they were leaving the restaurant, Pete laughed and said, "I should've known."

Tommie looked at him in confusion. "I beg your pardon?"

She followed his gaze to a handsome man approaching them. Pete stepped forward and gave him a hug and then said, "Tommie, I'd like you to meet my twin, Jim."

His *twin?* Now Tommie knew Pete Schofield was definitely not The One.

Chapter Two

Pete really knew something was wrong with Tommie. She was quiet during the remainder of lunch, but he'd chalked that up to preoccupation. After all, he knew she was determined to find him the perfect place to live. But when they got to the first house, she seemed less enthusiastic. She ushered him in and let him look around on his own while she made a few phone calls. She made sure she was never in the same room as he.

The house was too cramped and older than he wanted, but Tommie didn't ask what he thought. She simply took him to the next house, where they followed the same routine. When they left, he suggested they have coffee somewhere and discuss what he'd liked and disliked about the homes. More importantly, he wanted to discuss what was suddenly wrong with her.

"Certainly, if you think that would help," she responded.

No encouragement there.

"Here's a Starbucks. Is that okay?"

She nodded and pulled her car into a parking place. When they were settled at a table with cups of specialized coffee in front of them, Pete got right down to business.

"What's wrong? Have you decided to not sell me a house?"

"No, of course not. I'm sorry if I seemed a little preoccupied today. I didn't— I have something on my mind." She pulled a tablet out of her purse. "Now, what did you not like about those two homes?"

He mentioned several things, but his mind was still stuck on her change of behavior. The more he thought about it, she seemed to have become withdrawn right after he'd introduced her to Jim at the restaurant. "What did you think of my brother?"

"He seemed nice."

"He's great. I've missed him a lot."

"So why aren't you moving in with him?"

He frowned. "We're both grown men. I hope to start a family. Why wouldn't I buy my own house?"

"Does he have his own house?"

"No. He's in a condo. I'm not sure what he's planning for the future." Pete took a sip of coffee, watching

Tommie out of the corner of his eye. She gave no discernible sign that she disliked or disapproved of Jim.

He put down the cup and decided to be blunt. "It seemed to me that you were upset about meeting my brother. I just wondered why."

"No, not at all. In fact, I could introduce one of my sisters to him, if you want."

"You have sisters?"

"Yes, two."

"I didn't know. Do they resemble you?" he asked, unable to think about three Tommies. One was doing strange things to him. "What are their names?"

"Tabitha and Teresa."

"Tommie, Tabitha and Teresa? Three T's?" Pete asked.

His question didn't win a happy response.

"We're a little tired of that."

"Sorry, I just thought— Well, sometimes parents don't use the best judgment in naming their children. I was really grateful that my mother didn't— Well, you know how twins get named sometimes. Jim and I were treated as individuals."

Tommie made no response.

"How old are your sisters?"

Ignoring his question, she said, "Shall I tell you about the houses you'll see tomorrow?"

Pete frowned. "You don't want to talk about your sisters?"

She shook her head. "We have a lot of work to do.

Now, will you have the entire day free tomorrow to see more houses?"

"Yeah. I'd really hoped I would find a place right away. After all, you'll be working for my staff next week. I'm flying in the wives, too."

"I know. I've actually talked to a couple of them. I have everything planned out."

"I'm sure you do. So what do you have set up tomorrow for me?"

She pulled some pages out of her bag. "Here are five houses I think you'll like."

He looked at the pictures and read the information. "Do you like any of these?"

"Well, they all have things I like. They're not perfect, but then no house—or person—is."

"Okay, we'll look at them." He gave her back the papers. "What are you doing tonight?"

"Tonight?" She stared at him, surprised. "I—I need to look for more houses."

"All work and no play is bad for anyone, Tommie. Why don't you let me take you to dinner." Before she could answer, he snapped his fingers. "I just got a great idea. You can ask your sisters and I'll bring Jim and—and someone else. All six of us will go out to dinner. It'll be great."

"I don't know if my sisters are free. And I don't think we should mix business and pleasure."

"Nonsense! Call your sisters now. Are they at work?"

"No. They're both teachers."

He could tell she was still resistant. He wasn't an egotist, but he knew he was fairly good-looking. He'd never had any difficulty getting dates. Not that he'd done much dating in Boston. Starting your own business didn't leave much time. And after his company was established, it took all his concentration to run. About the only times he'd asked a woman out were to the business and charitable functions he was required to attend. Then the women seemed more than happy to be his date; many hinted they wanted more than one night. So why, then, was Tommie reluctant?

He pressed her. "Call them, Tommie…please?"

After studying him for a minute, she took out her cell phone and dialed a number. "Teresa? It's Tommie. Mr. Schofield, my client, has offered dinner for the three of us with him, his brother and a friend tonight. Can you make it?"

After she paused for her sister's answer, she added, "And Tab?"

Another pause. Then, "Okay, I'll let you know time and place later."

"They agreed?" Pete asked when she flipped her phone shut.

"Teresa agreed, and she said Tabitha would, too, but she's making an exercise video for teenagers, so I couldn't talk to her."

"Making a video? Is she going to market it?"

"Yes, she hopes to. And she'll use it in her own classes."

"I gather she's a P.E. teacher."

Tommie nodded.

"And Teresa? What does she teach?"

"Kindergarten. She loves it."

"That's terrific. They both sound like they're doing what makes them happy." And so was he—going out on a date with Tommie Tyler.

Pete had chosen an expensive restaurant, one Tommie and her sisters had only been to once. Last year, for their mother's birthday.

Tommie was at Tabitha's place, waiting for her sister to finish primping after getting home late.

"I'm excited about this evening," Tabitha said as she came out of the bathroom.

"I hope it's enjoyable," Tommie said. She couldn't keep the qualms from her voice. Though she had no clear reason, she feared the dinner was going to be a disaster. She should've held her ground when she told Pete their time together should be for business only.

Teresa studied her sister. "You sound worried. What's wrong, Tommie? Don't you like the man? You said you thought he was The One."

"He's not," she replied quickly and succinctly. "I was wrong."

"Why?" Tabitha asked.

Reluctantly she said, "He's looking for a nester. You know," she added when her sisters looked confused. "Someone who loves to make a home, wants to spend her time pregnant and barefoot in the kitchen. That's not me."

"Did he say that?"

"Not in so many words, but he's looking for a big house to fill with lots of kids."

"So he's engaged?" Tabitha asked.

"No."

Teresa said quietly, "Maybe you're misjudging him."

"I don't think so. Besides—" Tommie bit her tongue, not wanting to reveal too much of her feelings.

"Besides what?" Tabitha demanded, sounding impatient with her sister's worries.

"He's a twin," Tommie blurted out.

"Oh," Tabitha said.

"What's wrong with that?" Teresa wanted to know.

Just about everything, Tommie said to herself. Combine her propensity for multiple births with Pete's... She shuddered at the thought. "If I ever decide to have children, I want to have them one at a time," she said flatly. She crossed the room and hugged both sisters. "You two are great, but don't you remember how crowded the bathroom was? And how we shared our clothes? None of us knew what was whose or if it would be in the closet when we needed it."

"I kind of miss those days," Teresa said with a smile.

Tabitha concurred. "Yeah, we had fun, didn't we? But poor Mom!"

"Exactly. That's my point," Tommie explained. "I'm going to have a career first. And then I'll have one baby at a time."

"But sometimes you meet someone who's perfect.

You can't let him go by without trying to find out what your relationship is," Teresa said.

"I don't believe there's only one man for each woman. If I pass him by, it doesn't mean I'll be a spinster all my life."

"Let's not have this argument tonight," Tabitha interjected. "Besides, there's no time. How does my hair look?"

She wore her hair down to her shoulders, the ends turned under. Teresa had taken her hair out of its customary braid and it flowed halfway down her back, with the sides pulled away in combs. Tommie sometimes regretted cutting her own hair so short, but the chic style suited her. "You look beautiful, Tab. Both of you do."

"And so do you." Tabitha giggled. "Imagine us going on a triple date. Why didn't we ever do this when we were teenagers?"

Tommie knew the answer to that: because it would've been a disaster. Just like tonight was going to be. She let the question hang there, unanswered. Instead, she ushered her sisters out the door.

"I told Pete we would meet them at the restaurant." She hadn't wanted to give Pete control over when she arrived and left.

All three got in Tommie's Lexus.

"You know, Tab, when you sell your video, you'll be able to afford a car like this. Then I'll be the only one without a nice car," Teresa said.

"I use my car as an extension of my office, Teresa.

That's why I have to have a nice one," Tommie said, almost apologetically. She made a lot more money than her sisters and at times it bothered her. Though she was always more than generous. Often she bought three of an item, telling her sisters the bargain was too good to pass up.

As they neared the restaurant, Tommie could feel her nerves start to rattle. By the time she pulled in to the lot, she was ready to turn around and run. But that wasn't her style. She sat there for a moment, gathering her composure, until the valet approached.

"What's wrong?" Teresa asked.

"Nothing," she replied. "Let's go." All three got out of the car, and from the valet's look, she knew they made quite a picture together. After all, they'd been triplets all their lives. They caused a stir everywhere they went.

Which was exactly the problem. She should've told Pete.

Pete sat there staring at the door of the restaurant.

His brother interrupted his vigil. "I've never seen you like this, Pete. You stuck on this woman?" Jim asked.

"You saw Tommie. What do you think?" Pete returned, smiling at his brother.

"This is the real-estate lady?" the third man asked. He was one of the executives moving to Fort Worth. A single guy, he'd come early to get settled.

"Yeah, Brett. She's gorgeous, and successful. If her sisters look anything like her—"

Just then, Pete caught sight of Tommie. "There she is."

All three men turned toward the door.

Brett agreed with Pete's assessment of the lady named Tommie. Jim was about to agree when a second…and then a third Tommie came into view. The women were identical, tall, slim, blond. Only their hairstyles were different.

Jim spoke first. "What the hell, Pete? You didn't tell us they were triplets."

"That's because Tommie didn't tell me." Pete got up from the table and walked over to greet the ladies.

"Good evening. I'm Pete Schofield," he said to Tommie's sisters. Then, "Tommie, would you do the introductions?"

She motioned with her hand. "This is Tabitha and this is Teresa. May I present Mr. Peter Schofield."

"Make it Pete." He smiled and pointed over his shoulder. "We're at a table over here." He took Tommie's arm and led them to the table. On the way he whispered, "Why didn't you tell me you were triplets?"

"Does it matter?" Tommie asked coolly.

Pete frowned, but they'd reached the table and he introduced the ladies to Jim and Brett. Both men had stood as the ladies approached.

They all sat down, alternating man, woman. Brett was on Tommie's left and Pete wasn't pleased when Tommie began a conversation with his old friend and employee. Tabitha was talking to Jim, which left Teresa, on the other side of Brett, and himself without anyone to talk to.

When Brett turned to Teresa, Pete immediately drew Tommie's attention. "You two talking about housing?"

"Yes. He's going to look at all the condos I had lined up for you."

"Good. Who's going to show them to him? I mean, we planned on seeing houses tomorrow."

"I told him I could work him in tomorrow after lunch. After all, it hasn't taken you that long to look at the houses I've shown you. I'm sure tomorrow won't be any different."

"Are you upset that it's taking me some time to find a house? I expected it to be quicker, but I just haven't seen what I want."

"I'm taking you to more modern homes tomorrow. That is what you want, isn't it?"

"Yes, it is." Before he could say more, they were interrupted by the arrival of their waiter. After they all ordered, Pete tried to keep the conversation more general. He asked the women about their careers.

Tabitha launched enthusiastically into her story, but Teresa was more reluctant to talk about her teaching. Tommie encouraged her to tell several funny stories about her kindergarten students.

By the time dinner was over, Pete realized he'd learned nothing more about Tommie, as he'd hoped. Especially what was bothering her. He tried to extend the evening with dancing at Billy Bob's, a famous cowboy bar downtown, but Tommie begged off, citing some more work, and after thanking Pete for dinner, the triplets left.

In Pete's car, the three men were silent for the first few minutes. Then Brett said, "All three sisters are beautiful. Don't you think so, Jim?"

"Sure. I met Tommie earlier today, so I didn't expect any of them to be ugly, but I also didn't expect them to be triplets."

"Neither did I," Pete agreed.

"So, Tommie's the one you're interested in?" Brett asked, his voice casual.

"That's right. Why? You interested in one of them?"

"I was impressed with Tabitha. She said I could come watch her make the video tomorrow." Brett turned to Jim. "What did you think of Teresa?"

"She seemed nice, but I couldn't date her. We'd never have any conversation between us. She was as quiet as me."

Brett laughed and Pete couldn't help smiling. "That's not true, Jim. You can talk about a lot. You just don't like to compete for time. With Teresa, you'd have all the time you need."

"Yeah, too much."

"Well, I appreciate the introduction to Tabitha. When you move into a new city, sometimes it's hard to make connections," Brett said. "I'm looking forward to seeing her film the video. I bet she wears one of those spandex outfits."

That was the wrong thing to say. From that point on, all Pete could do was envision Tommie as the exercise guru, wearing bright red spandex and bending over to touch her toes.

The next morning was as unsuccessful as the previous house hunting. Only the kitchen in one home piqued any interest in Pete. Tommie admitted the room was lovely, but Pete's questions didn't change her feelings toward him.

"What's the first meal you'd cook in this kitchen?" he asked, standing at the center island.

She stiffened. Then she said, "Chinese takeout."

"Come on, Tommie, I said cook."

"I don't cook, Pete. I seldom eat at home. If I do, I put a frozen dinner in the microwave or make a sandwich."

"Tommie, I'm sure you can cook something."

He obviously didn't get her point. She was just not a homemaker. She decided to turn the tables. "And what would you cook, Pete?"

"*I* don't cook."

"Then we have something in common," she said and strolled out of the kitchen.

Frowning, he came after her. "But, Tommie, you're a woman."

"How true. And your point?"

"Well, women should— I mean, my mother is a great cook."

"Lucky for you."

"Is your mom a good cook?"

"Not particularly. Since my father died before we were born, she had to work outside the home. Dinners weren't elegant or well planned. But she took good care of us."

"I'm sure she did." He said nothing else until they were in the car. "How did your dad die?"

"He was a fireman. The roof of a burning building fell in on him and another fireman. They weren't able to get out." She kept the story short. Though she missed having a father growing up, there was no point sharing those emotions with her client. And that was all Pete Schofield would ever be.

She stuck to business. "The next house also has a nice kitchen. And a study. There are only three bedrooms, however."

"Then let's not waste my time. I only want four bedrooms or larger. Don't you have something nicer?"

"I do, but I can't show it until next Monday. The builder has one or two things to fix. He's a perfectionist. He let the Realtors go through it last week, but he told us we couldn't show the home until Monday. It's the most marvelous house. Brand-new, with four bedrooms, each with its own bath, another bath downstairs, a study, den, large living room and dining room and a futuristic kitchen."

"Sounds perfect. Let's not look at any more houses until you can show me that one."

"All right, but I must warn you it's a little pricey." She named the asking price. "Of course, we can counter with a lower price and he might take it."

"We'll decide that after I see the house."

"All right. Do you want me to take you back to your mother's, or is there somewhere else I can drop you?" Tommie was feeling a mixture of regret and relief.

"Let's go to lunch first. I've got some ideas I'd like to discuss with you. You have time for lunch before you take Brett around, don't you? You have to eat, after all."

Tommie paused before she said, "I can go to lunch with you, but I don't know how I can help you other than find you a house."

"I'll explain. It will be painless, I promise."

After they were seated in a nearby restaurant and had ordered their meals, he said, "I want to introduce my staff and their spouses to the area, show them some benefits of being here. So I thought I'd start Monday night by leasing a suite at the Texas Rangers game."

"That's a lovely idea."

"Good, I'm glad you like it. I'd like you to come and act as my hostess. It will give you a chance to visit with the wives on a casual basis. You can tell them about the area."

"I think your taking them out is a good idea, Pete, but I don't think I should be the one to play hostess for you. I'm sure your mother would do a good job in that role."

"I love my mother, but she would have nothing in

common with these ladies. The wives are younger and wouldn't have much interest in the local bridge club."

Tommie sighed. "I don't know, Pete. It doesn't seem right."

"Do you want me to pay you? Is that the problem?"

"No! I wasn't trying to get more money out of you. I'll make plenty selling houses to all your staff and you."

"And your being the hostess means you'll do a more efficient job finding what each lady is looking for in a house. Do you hate baseball?"

"No, I enjoy watching the Rangers play."

"Well, then? After all, you won't have to do any cooking."

Tommie's gaze narrowed. She'd vowed to avoid any social contact with Pete, but after all, this was actually business. She nodded her head. "Fine, I accept."

Chapter Three

The rest of the week flew by. The third condo Tommie showed Brett pleased him. He put in an offer and it was accepted. In addition, Tommie had a closing on an earlier sale. In the meantime, she researched various homes on the market, trying to match each couple transferring with five or six possible choices.

Pete called her several times to check on her progress. He offered to take her out to dinner to celebrate selling the condo to Brett, but she refused. The man was too attractive to her and she knew only total avoidance would be effective. They were simply not a good fit.

Her sisters were having similar experiences. Tabitha had gone out with Brett several times, but Tommie was pretty sure she wasn't falling for him. Jim, meanwhile, hadn't even called Teresa.

By Saturday, Tommie regretted having agreed to the baseball game. She found out Brett had invited Tabitha, which left Teresa as odd man out.

She was sitting in Teresa's kitchen, watching her bake cookies and sampling a few along the way, when the phone rang. Teresa answered the kitchen extension. "Hello?"

Tommie figured it was their mother calling. But the encroaching blush on her sister's cheeks made Tommie change her mind.

"Why, I'd love to. I enjoy baseball."

Tommie's gaze narrowed. Could this be Jim? Neither Tabitha nor Tommie had mentioned their plans for Monday night, afraid it would upset Teresa not to be included.

When Teresa hung up the phone, she asked, "Why didn't you tell me about the baseball-game party?"

"Brett had invited Tabitha and I didn't want you to get your feelings hurt if Jim didn't call."

Teresa crossed to Tommie's side and hugged her. "Silly. I have dates on occasion. I don't sit at home all the time."

"Of course not, but…well, I'm glad we'll all three be there Monday night."

"Yes. You haven't said how things have been going with Pete's house search."

"He wants to wait until Monday when I can show him a brand-new house. It's pretty pricey, but that didn't seem to bother him."

"Good. When do the other people come in?"

"Actually, that's the reason for the trip to the ball-park. It's their first evening in Fort Worth. Pete wants to show them the advantages to the area."

"That's good. Are they taking the kids to Six Flags Over Texas?"

"The kids aren't coming this week. But when they move here, that would be a good thing to organize for them." Tommie absentmindedly picked up another cookie to munch on as she said, "I thought I'd recommend an evening at the new symphony hall. It's so beautiful."

"Casa is open again, isn't it?" Teresa asked, naming a theater-in-the-round that had been in Fort Worth for many years.

"Good idea. I'll recommend that, too. And the PGA tournament at the Colonial Golf Course is next week, too. The guys would probably enjoy a day at the tournament, and the ladies could do a luncheon on the same day, probably Friday," Tommie said.

"I bet that's more than enough activities for them. Then, after they all move, I'd be glad to take them to Six Flags or to the zoo. Little ones are my specialty, after all."

"Yes, they are. You have a great calming effect on children. I'll suggest that to Pete."

As if she conjured him, Pete called her cell phone.

"My mother invited you to dinner this evening," he said. "She's excited to have you over."

Tommie was instantly concerned with what he

might've told his mother. Not wanting to sound ungracious, she nevertheless asked, "Why?"

"Because I've talked about you a lot." Before she could protest and decline, he added, "And Jim wanted to invite Teresa, too."

Great. Now she'd have to go. She wouldn't begrudge her sister the night out with Jim.

She covered the receiver and asked Teresa, who was thrilled with the suggestion.

"We'll be there," Tommie reluctantly reported. Then, as if to salve her conscience, she said, "We've been thinking about things you should do for your staff and their spouses. We'll tell you tonight."

"Great. I'll pick you up at—"

"No, I'll drive us."

"Tommie, I should come pick you up."

"No, thank you. We'll manage."

"Fine. Seven o'clock."

After hanging up the phone, Tommie confessed, "I think he's invited me to dinner so I can see how well his mother cooks."

"Why would you think that?" Teresa asked.

"When I was showing him a house with a beautiful kitchen he wanted to know what I would cook first in that kitchen. I explained I didn't cook."

"Tommie, that's not true. You can cook a lot of things."

"Yes, but I'm not a cook like you are. Or even Mom."

"So you told him you wouldn't cook anything?"

"No, I said I'd order Chinese takeout."

Teresa gasped. "You didn't!"

"I did. He might as well know up front that I'm not the type of woman he's interested in."

"I suppose you're right about that," Teresa replied. She was. Wasn't she?

That evening, when Pete introduced Teresa and Tommie to his mother, Evelyn Schofield clapped her hands in delight. "You didn't tell me they were twins, Peter."

"We're not," Tommie said hurriedly. "We're triplets. Our sister, Tabitha, isn't here tonight."

"Oh, how amazing. I thought I had my hands full with twins. However did your mother manage?"

"It wasn't easy, especially since she held down a full-time job," Tommie said.

"She did? Oh my, I didn't want to work. My first priority was my children."

Teresa and Tommie remained silent. It was Pete who explained to his mother. "Their father died before they were born. Their mother didn't have a choice, Mom."

"Oh my, how sad."

Jim looked at Teresa. "I didn't know that, Teresa."

She shrugged her shoulders. "It happened a long time ago."

"Tommie is such a strange name for a girl. How did you end up with that?" Mrs. Schofield asked.

Tommie gritted her teeth. She hated that question.

Teresa answered for her. "Mom wanted to have a son

and name him after Dad. But she had three girls. So she named the oldest Thomasina, after Dad, who was named Thomas. Then she found T names for the rest of us."

"Ah, I see. Does that make life difficult for you, Tommie?"

Tommie lifted her chin. "Not at all."

"A gorgeous blonde like these two and their sister could use any name and make everyone happy," Jim said quietly, almost reprimanding his mother.

"Well, of course, I didn't mean—"

"We knew you didn't, Mrs. Schofield," Tommie said, trying to smooth the conversation. "I'm looking forward to dinner. Pete has told me what a wonderful cook you are."

"Oh, yes. My husband and I used to enjoy giving dinner parties. I've used the same caterer for years."

Tommie almost choked. "A—a caterer?"

"Yes. I'll give you their name if you want."

"Mom, I thought you cooked everything," Pete said, surprise in his words.

"Dear, I can't look beautiful *and* do the cooking. Just like having the house cleaned by our maid before I entertain. I can do one of the three, but no one could do all three." She smiled serenely at the two young women, no doubt in her demeanor.

Tommie fought to hold back laughter as Pete stared at his mother as if he didn't know her. He shot Jim a speaking look, but Jim just shrugged his shoulders.

As they sat down to dinner, Tommie complimented her hostess on the beauty of the table.

"Oh, thank you, dear. My darling husband bought me this china when we were in France on holiday before the boys were born. I do so love it."

Mrs. Schofield went on to tell them where she'd found the stemware and silver that matched it so well. They were halfway through the meal before she took a breath.

Pete hurriedly asked about the plans Tommie and Teresa had discussed for his employees.

Pete liked all the ideas, especially the golf tournament.

"Thanks, Teresa. I want my people to be happy here."

"Are they all native Bostonians?" Tommie asked.

"No, but they're all from the Northeast. Life is a little different there."

"Jim, did you go away to college, too?" Teresa asked.

He smiled. "No, Dad had just died, and I thought I should stay close to home. I lived on campus, but I went to Texas Christian here in the city. I was nearby if Mom needed anything."

"You're a thoughtful person," Teresa said with a smile.

"Of course he is," Evelyn gushed. "Both of my sons are wonderful. Pete called me quite a bit, too, even though he was so far away. But he'd been awarded a scholarship to Harvard. I didn't want him to miss that opportunity."

"Jim had a scholarship to TCU, too," Pete reminded his mother.

"Yes, of course, and that worked out well for me."

"I'm sure it did," Tommie agreed, exchanging a knowing smile with her sister.

"Those were very nice young ladies," Evelyn commented after Tommie and Teresa had departed.

"Yes, they are," Jim agreed.

"I'm surprised that they had such nice manners, since their mother worked. Career women don't think about how their jobs affect their children." She gave a self-satisfied nod.

"Mom," Pete began, "not every woman has a choice about working. You were fortunate that Dad was well insured and that he'd inherited a lot of money and property from his father."

"Yes, but some women work even when they don't have to, and I think it penalizes their husband and children when they do."

Jim shook his head at his brother when Pete opened his mouth to try again to explain to his mother the realities of modern life.

Instead, Jim kissed his mother's cheek and thanked her for a lovely dinner. Then he said he needed to go because he had some things to do.

Pete quickly followed his example. Both young men stepped outside at the same time.

"Got time for a cup of coffee?" Pete asked.

"Sure. Where shall we go?"

Pete named a coffee shop nearby and they agreed to meet there.

Pete got into his car, but his mind was on the conversation at dinnertime. When he and his brother had settled into a booth and ordered their coffee, he said, "I didn't realize Mom used a caterer when she entertained."

"There's a lot you don't realize about Mom. Dad spoiled her a lot. When he died and you went away to school, I filled in as companion, car mechanic, lightbulb changer and errand runner."

The waitress brought their coffee. Jim took a drink before he added, "I also was the one to call the plumber, the handyman, and the man who mowed the grass. Mom didn't want to deal with those people."

"Why?"

"Because Dad always dealt with those things. She expected her life to remain the same even though he was gone."

"Damn it, why didn't you say something? You must hate me now," Pete said with regret.

"If I'd called and complained, you would've given up Harvard and hurried home so *you* could make those calls and run errands. Then you'd hate *me*."

"No, but at least I would've appreciated you more."

"That's all right. You served a purpose. Mom could brag that one of her sons went to Harvard."

"TCU is a good school, too. And you've done very well for yourself, becoming a partner so early."

"Being a CPA isn't as sexy as being president of your own company." He held up a hand when Pete would've protested. "I'm not complaining. I'm happy with my job and my life. I'm just telling you how Mom thinks."

"I'm sorry, Jim."

Jim grinned. "Don't worry. You're going to make up for the past ten or so years. Now that her impressive son has returned home, she's going to demand your presence at every dinner or party she gives. You'll be trotted out so many times you'll feel like throwing up. And the matchmaking! You're a prize catch, and she's going to expect you to marry the daughter of an industry giant, or, even better, someone with royal connections."

Pete felt as if he was going to lose his dinner already. "I hope you're wrong."

Jim said nothing, but Pete could tell from his grim smile that he was sure he was right.

"So you don't think Tommie would receive her approval?"

"Get real, bro. Didn't you hear her say that she was amazed that they had good manners? Tommie wouldn't have a chance."

Pete frowned. Then, looking at his brother from under lowered lashes, he said, "Tommie doesn't cook."

"Neither does Mom, but that wouldn't stop her from condemning Tommie."

"Well, I think a woman should be able to cook. If her husband wants to throw a dinner party, she should be able to play hostess."

"Did you tell Tommie that?"

"I—I hinted that I expected my wife to cook."

"Do you cook?" Jim asked.

"I don't starve to death, but most of my meals are taken in restaurants."

"I imagine hers are, too."

"Yeah, she said that's something we have in common."

Jim laughed. "She's a strong woman. I think her sisters are, too. And they all seem happy with their jobs."

"I suppose so."

"If you want a woman trained to make a home for you and any future children, you're looking for a woman like Mom. But you pay a price for such limited outlook."

"So you're not looking for a woman like Mom?" Pete asked, curiosity in his voice.

"I can't afford the time for two women like that. I want a woman who can do things for herself. Who can do things for me if I get in a crunch, and vice versa, but who can stand on her own two feet."

"And what happens when you have children?"

"We'll work things out. I don't think it's only the woman who raises the children."

"Well, no, of course not, but… You plan on changing diapers?"

"Why should that only be a woman's job?"

"Doing laundry, cooking, taking care of the kids? You're going to share all that?"

Jim laughed. "Man, you've got to move into the twenty-first century! I hope I have enough money to hire a maid or housekeeper to help with everything, but why have children if you're not going to raise them?"

"I guess you're right. Dad spent a lot of time with us."

"Yes, he did. Don't you remember Mom saying we were too rambunctious to stay in the house? She always expected Dad to take us out. She'd wave her hand and say, 'Take them outside. I have a headache.'"

Pete gave his brother a rueful grin. "Yeah, I do remember."

"In her mind, she spent all her free time with us. But in reality, she spent a lot of time at the club with her friends."

"Wow! You've given me a lot to think about."

"Here's a little more for your edification. Remember Greg Bowden?"

"Sure. We all went to high school together. He went to Stanford, didn't he?"

"Yeah. Got his law degree. He married Suzanne Gaston, the blonde we all had a crush on."

"Yeah, I remember her. She resembles Tommie and her sisters a little."

"Yeah. Well, you should hear Greg when we play golf. He's angry and frustrated because he didn't realize how that kind of woman makes marriage difficult. She calls him out of meetings because she wants him to come home and babysit their child because the babysitter can't come and she wants to go out shopping."

"Not good. How does he deal with it?"

"Not well. He says his charge bills are stacking up, but she insists she's only buying what she really needs. He says she has more than fifty pairs of shoes. And she's still shopping."

"Does Mom do that?"

Jim just shook his head. "Check out her closet sometimes. She has clothes she's bought and never worn. The price tag is still on them from ten years ago. But she still goes shopping. Fortunately for us, Dad left her a lot of money, but I wouldn't count on any inheritance."

"Isn't there anything we can do?"

"Dad let her spend what she wanted. And now she spends because she has nothing else to do." Jim shook his head. "And that's exactly why I want a woman who takes care of herself, who has learned to live on a budget and who has interests other than her husband's income."

"And you haven't found one of those yet?" Pete asked.

"I haven't been in a hurry because I had Mom on my hands. But we're thirty-one now. I think it's time I do some serious looking. I don't want to be too old when I have kids."

"True, but my company still needs a lot of my time to keep it growing. I don't see how I can be the kind of dad and husband you're talking about and do that."

Jim nodded. "I think it's a matter of priorities. I'm ready to put first a relationship and any children that come along. I'd advise you not to marry until you're ready to do the same. Or at least until you've spent a while tending to our mother. Then you'll understand better what I mean."

Pete nodded. Jim had given him a lot to think about. But surely he was exaggerating. At least, Pete hoped so.

Chapter Four

On Monday morning, Tommie picked up Pete again at nine o'clock. But they weren't going out for a leisurely breakfast. Pete was intent on being the first person to look at the new house.

Tommie had already talked to the builder to be sure the house had a lockbox and that it was ready to be shown. The man had assured her that was true. He added that he'd had a lot of calls about it.

When she casually passed on that information, Pete glared at her.

"I don't respond well to threats!"

Tommie turned to stare at him until he grabbed the wheel, righting the direction of the car. "Pay attention," he snapped.

"What are you talking about?" she demanded, keeping her eyes forward. "I didn't threaten you!"

"No, you're just trying to put pressure on me to make a rush buy."

She turned on her blinker and took the first right turn. Before Pete realized it, she had made the block and had them going back toward his mother's house.

"What are you doing?" he demanded.

"Taking you back to your mother's. I don't do business the way you've implied. The only way to prove that is to refuse to show you the house today. Tomorrow will be fine."

"You're being absurd! I want to see the house today."

"You don't respond well to threats? I don't respond well to insults and bullying. Maybe you should get another Realtor altogether."

"That will take too much time, Ms. Tyler. Turn this car around and take me to see that house!"

She hesitated. Finally she did as he asked, saying nothing to him. When they finally reached their target, there was another car parked in front of the house. Tommie recognized it as belonging to a fellow Realtor. But she didn't share that information with Pete. She wasn't going to be accused of "threatening" him again.

"Is the builder meeting us here?" Pete asked.

"No."

"Then, whose car is that?"

Tommie raised one eyebrow. "You expect me to recognize every car in Fort Worth?"

"No, but—"

"But what? I brought you here like you asked. Don't you think we should go in? Or are you going to make your decision from the sidewalk?"

She looked down her nose at him, challenging him to do just that. Not that she'd take an offer to the builder without Pete seeing the house, but she wanted to know just how stubborn he was.

"I want to see the house," he said firmly.

She didn't think he'd even consider buying it after this morning, but her duty was to show the property. "Very well. Let's go in."

They followed the winding sidewalk to the front door. The builder had beautifully landscaped the lot and it was impressive. The lockbox was open, so Tommie tried the door. It opened at once.

"Someone's in here?" Pete asked.

"Yes, I believe so, but you can still look at the house."

They entered and a young brunette woman spun around. "Tommie! How are you? I missed you at the last Realtors' meeting."

"Hi, Shelly. No, I didn't make it." She turned to Pete and introduced him to her fellow Realtor. Then she asked, "Do you want me to go through the house with you, or do you prefer to wander around on your own?" she asked politely.

"I'll manage," he said grimly.

After he'd walked away, Shelly raised her eyebrows and nodded in Pete's direction. "In a bad mood?"

"Yes," Tommie said with a sigh.

"Too bad. He's handsome."

"Yes. Are your clients wandering through?"

"You bet. I heard there was a lot of interest in this house, so I got them here early."

"Is this their first house? To look at, I mean."

Shelly nodded. "Yeah. I should've taken them to some of the other listings so they'd have a point of comparison, but I was afraid this place would be snapped off the market if I wasted time."

"I'm not sure if the builder was yanking our chains, hoping to get a fast sale," Tommie said with another sigh.

"I bet he will. This is my favorite house."

"Mine, too," Tommie said as a couple came down the winding staircase.

"Well, what do you think?" Shelly asked as the pair reached the first floor.

"A bit pricey," the man said.

"I'm sorry. I thought I told you the price before we came here." Shelly had stiffened at his words.

"You did, but for that much money, I expected a palace," he said with a shrug.

Tommie turned away so the people wouldn't see her grin. They obviously hadn't looked at the market before they started their search. When she talked to Pete, he knew exactly what the market was. Of course, his mother and brother still lived here.

"Well, there's another house in the neighborhood

that you might like better. Why don't we go check it out," Shelly said with forced cheerfulness.

With a nod to Tommie, she escorted her clients out the door.

"Are they gone?" Pete asked from behind her.

Tommie shrieked as she spun around. She hadn't heard him enter the hall. "Yes, they're gone."

"And they're not interested in the house?"

"I don't think so."

"Good. I want it."

Tommie stared at him. "Have you even been upstairs?"

"No, but—"

"There's no way I'm taking an offer to the builder until you've looked at the entire house."

She took his arm and began a formal tour, not allowing him to say anything. Marching him up the stairs, she carefully showed him each bedroom and all four baths. She even insisted he go out on the balcony off the master bedroom.

"Now that you've seen all the house, you can go back and look at anything you want to see again. I'll wait for you downstairs."

He grabbed her arm to stop her. "Tommie, I—"

They both heard the door open downstairs. "Hello?" someone called out.

In an undertone, Pete said, "I want the house. Put in an offer at once."

"We have to discuss what you want to offer," Tommie whispered.

"The asking price. I don't want to lose the house trying to talk him out of a few thousand."

"Okay. We'll go to the car. I can call Mr. Hanson from there."

They went down the stairs where another Realtor greeted Tommie before she began a tour of the house with her clients.

Tommie kept a hand on Pete's arm, afraid he might tell them he'd bought the house. And that wasn't true—yet.

When they reached the car, she got in and took out her cell phone. Dialing Mr. Hanson's number, she told him she had an offer at the asking price.

"Type it up and bring it to me."

"So you'll accept it?" she asked, hearing something in the builder's voice that worried her.

"I'll let you know. I'm expecting several offers today."

Tommie dreaded hanging up the phone. How was she going to tell Pete the house wasn't his?

It was still early in the season, so the Texas Rangers' devoted fans had hopes of a better season. The stands were rapidly filling for the Monday-night game.

Tommie and Teresa had been picked up by Pete and his brother. On the way to the ballpark, Pete asked about his contract, but all Tommie could say was there was no word yet.

"You're not going to show that house to any of my people, are you?"

"No, of course not," she said and changed the subject.

They arrived early to be on hand to greet all their guests. Tommie already knew the names of everyone who would be attending, as well as a few things about their preferences and their families, but she was looking forward to meeting them in person.

The suite contained tables and chairs, enough for a dozen people. There were several televisions and wide windows in the front of the suite that could be opened. It overlooked the baseball field a little to the first-base side.

Teresa turned to Jim. "We'll have a great view here."

"Yeah. I'm glad you like baseball."

"Mostly I watch it on television, but I try to make it to the ballpark a couple of times a year. There's such a wonderful atmosphere here."

"My people are going to be comparing it to Fenway Park and the Green Monster," Pete said, referring to the Boston Red Sox's stadium with a very high outfield wall painted green.

"Well, we don't have the history of Fenway, but our stadium is beautiful," Tommie pointed out.

"I hope it makes them happy," Pete said.

"You don't think anyone will change their minds because of a baseball stadium, do you?" Tommie asked, incredulity in her voice.

"Some people are dedicated fans," was his only comment.

The first couple arrived and Pete introduced them. Of course, their reaction to Tommie and Teresa wasn't a surprise to the ladies. When Tabitha and Brett arrived next, they were amazed all over again.

Teresa whispered to Tommie, "I think we should stand together and get the reaction over with as quickly as possible."

"I know. Jim and Pete are twins, but since they're not identical, no one thinks anything about it."

Tabitha joined her sisters. "I'm getting a little tired of being stared at. I feel like I must have a big zit on my nose."

"No such luck. You're zit-free," Tommie assured her. "I know we all should be used to this now, but it's been a while since we appeared in public all together."

As people filtered in, the triplets tried to minimize their amazement, quickly greeting them and changing the subject. Tommie, in particular, grabbed their attention when she talked about their search for a nice home and the school district their children would be entering. Thankfully the buffet opened and Pete encouraged his friends to serve themselves.

"I like entertaining this way," Tabitha said quietly to her sisters.

"Yeah, it's easy, isn't it?" Teresa said.

"I thought you would prefer to do the cooking yourself," Tommie said to Teresa.

"I like to cook, but I'm no masochist," Teresa muttered before she filled a plate and settled at a table where Jim had saved her a seat.

Tabitha followed suit, only she joined Brett at another table.

Pete appeared beside Tommie just as the game was about to begin. "Everything going all right?"

Tommie nodded. "They all seem like nice people."

"They are. Otherwise, I wouldn't be moving them down here."

A cheer went up from the crowd and Tommie looked at the television screen. "Wow, did you see that? A home run on the first pitch! That's great! Look, even some of your people are cheering."

Pete grinned. "Sure they are. Texas is playing the Yankees. Red Sox fans always cheer against the Yankees."

With a laugh, Tommie nodded. "I should've remembered that. The Curse of the Babe."

"That's right. The Yankees stole Babe Ruth from the Sox and they've never forgotten that. But the curse is lifted now that Boston won a World Series."

"Have you filled a plate yet?" Tommie asked him.

"No, I was waiting on you." He indicated she should precede him. "We'll eat with Bill and Adele at the last table."

When they'd taken their places, Tommie greeted Adele, a brunette who appeared to be about ten years older than her. Then she said, "Adele, tell me about your children. You have two, don't you?"

Adele, like all mothers, loved that subject. She told Tommie about her two children, a boy and a girl, for several minutes. Then she said, "Oh, I've bored you long enough about my kids."

"Not at all," Tommie said. "It'll help me find a house that's right for you. In fact, I think I showed one to Pete last week that would be perfect for you. And it had a basketball hoop already up on the garage."

"Really? Tell me more about it."

"It has the most gorgeous kitchen. Pete was very impressed by it."

"I'm not sure that's a recommendation. We all know he doesn't even boil water."

Tommie laughed. "He wants a good kitchen for the wife he intends to have someday."

Adele rolled her eyes. "Typical man. I'm so lucky that Bill helps out at home."

"Glad to hear it. I thought maybe Pete's attitude was representative of society back East."

"You don't have men who think they are the superior race here in Texas?" Adele asked.

"We do, but we're trying to enlighten them as fast as we can," Tommie said with a laugh.

After dinner was over, the men pulled their chairs in front of the windows to focus on the game. Tommie took the opportunity to talk to the two other wives.

Since the executives had asked their wives to look at houses by themselves first, weeding out any they didn't like, Tommie promised to take the three women around on Tuesday. She knew it wasn't recommended to show the same houses to all of them, but she was confident they wouldn't be interested in the same things.

"You do know there will be two more couples in tomorrow, don't you?" Adele asked.

"No, I thought you were all coming in today."

"Two couples couldn't get away today. They're coming in tomorrow evening."

"Well, maybe you three will have found your houses by then," Tommie suggested.

"I don't like to make snap decisions," Patti Collins said, panic in her voice.

"Of course not, Patti. I wasn't suggesting you do anything until you're ready. But if you fall in love with a house, you might change your mind."

"I don't think so," Patti said firmly.

"I hope I find something I fall in love with," Adele said. "I want to get settled as soon as possible. My kids don't like change. They get that from their mother," she added with a rueful grin.

"I know," Tommie said. "Transitions are difficult for everyone. But that's what I'm here for. To make them easier."

She took that opportunity to tell the young mothers that Teresa was a kindergarten teacher and Tabitha taught aerobics at the high school. The women, who all had young children and had belonged to gyms back in Boston, were thrilled. They launched numerous questions at her sisters.

She was good, Tommie admitted to herself. Satisfied,

she sat back and grinned. Pete chose that very moment to look over at her and smile.

Now, if only she could fix her own problems that easily.

Bill leaned over to Pete. "Hey, your Tommie and her sisters are certainly good at making people feel at home."

"She's not *my* Tommie," Pete said. "I just met her when I was talking to the Realtor my mother recommended. Tommie works for her."

"You'd better claim her before someone else does," Bill said.

"I'm not sure she's what I'm looking for. She's not a homemaker."

"Neither was Adele when we first got married. But we both learned."

"Both?" Pete asked.

Bill clapped his boss on the back. "Forgive me for saying so, but for someone who knows everything about software and business," he said, stifling a laugh, "when it comes to women and marriage, you've got a lot to learn."

That was the second time in a week somebody had told him that. If he wasn't so self-confident, he'd start getting a complex.

"Let's have lunch one day this week and I'll bring you up to speed," Bill offered. "And once we get settled in our new house, you'll come over. Bring Tommie. Adele would like that."

"Yeah, they seem to get along well," he agreed, glancing at the two women who were once again chatting.

Pete realized Tommie had fulfilled his every expectation this evening. She'd played the role of hostess beautifully, making his guests feel welcome and relaxed, comfortable in what would be their new hometown. She was smart, sweet and savvy. And she was gorgeous.

The perfect woman. For some.

Despite what his brother, and Bill, had said, he believed it was the woman who made the difference in the home.

He mentally shook himself. He was worrying as if he were on the verge of proposing to Tommie. That, he assured himself, was never going to happen.

Just then a cheer rose from the crowd, drawing his attention back to the baseball game. The Rangers had a man rounding third and heading for home.

Chapter Five

Tommie had shuffled the women in and out of about seven houses the next day, stopping for only a brief lunch. Each of the ladies was making notes after every tour, as she'd suggested, fearing that after a while the houses would all start blurring together.

The only interruptions to the smooth flow of the day were the several calls Tommie received on her cell phone—all from Pete, wanting to know if she'd heard from the builder about the house.

Tommie was showing the ladies a newer ranch-style house when he called again.

"Is he holding out for more money?" Pete demanded.

She ignored his question. "I promised I'd call you as soon as I hear anything. Just relax." She didn't wait for him to sign off before she flipped her phone shut.

Patti shot her an amused look and Adele teased her. "Maybe Mr. Schofield is interested in more than just your real-estate skills."

"It's not that," Tommie assured them, blushing a little. "He's made an offer on a house and he's anxious to know if it's been accepted. If you'll look through the property on your own for a few minutes, I'll call the builder."

The ladies willingly started through the house while Tommie made the call.

"Mr. Hanson, this is Tommie Tyler again. My client is still waiting. Have you accepted his offer?"

"How about asking him to sweeten the pot a little?" the man suggested.

"If that's what you want, I'll certainly tell him. However, he's a very successful businessman. I suspect he'll choose another house."

There was silence on the line. Tommie waited him out.

Finally, the builder relented. "Okay, I'll take his offer. You can come by and pick up the contract. I'm signing it now. And I'm putting the earnest money in the bank today."

"I'll be there in fifteen minutes."

She put away her cell phone. She wanted to have the contract in hand before she informed Pete that he'd bought the house. The ladies returned to the foyer just then.

"Well, what did you think?"

All three of them shook their heads. Adele said,

"This is too much of a fixer-upper for us. One of the other couples likes to take on those challenges, but not us."

"All right. I need to go pick up a contract. Can each of you list the top two houses you think you're interested in while I'm driving?"

They agreed to do so. After they were settled in the car, they took out the sheet Tommie had given them with the sale price, brief description and address of each house.

They were still studying the list when Tommie stopped the car. "I'll be right back," she said, leaving the car running so the air-conditioning would keep her clients cool.

Inside, she looked over the contract. The builder reserved the right to continue showing the house until the closing, which was standard, though Tommie didn't think Pete would like it. But she took the contract and shook hands with Hanson.

When she reached the car, the ladies had their lists. Tommie looked at the lists and breathed a sigh of relief. They had all chosen a different house for their first choice. "I need to go to the new offices to take Pete his contract. Do you want to come along to see your husbands, or do you want to go back to the hotel?"

"The office," the ladies said in chorus.

"The office it is, then."

Five minutes later they parked in front of the building Pete had chosen for their offices. It was in the neighborhood where all the houses were located. The employees would have a five- or ten-minute drive to work, avoiding any traffic congestion.

"Which house did Pete pick?" one of the women asked.

"A brand-new home. I didn't show it to you because he'd already chosen it."

They laughed. "We definitely didn't want to be competing for a home with the boss. He's nice, but not that nice."

Tommie laughed along with the ladies. She was grateful she didn't have to disappoint him.

The locally hired receptionist told them that the men were in a meeting. Tommie asked if she could inform Mr. Schofield that she needed to see him.

The young woman appeared undecided. One of the wives stepped forward. "I can assure you, my dear, Pete will want to see Ms. Tyler."

The receptionist picked up the phone and passed on the message. The door to the conference room opened at once. Pete, with a frown on his face, searched for Tommie. When his gaze fell on her, he hurried forward.

"Tommie, what—"

She waved the contract at him. "You've bought a house!"

After a momentary frozen state, Pete rushed forward and picked her up by the waist, spinning around.

"Pete!" Tommie shrieked, surprised by his action.

He lowered her to the floor and gave her a smack on

the lips. There was nothing passionate or loving in his action. It was merely an impulsive celebration. Tommie understood his reaction, and she even enjoyed it.

Then his lips returned to hers, this time with passion, clinging, demanding a response. Tommie couldn't have pulled away if she'd wanted to. He held her firmly against him. But she didn't want to stop him. His lips held her captive, and she wasn't protesting.

Until a cheer went up.

Pete released her, in her mind reluctantly. Or maybe that was what she wanted to see.

He stepped away and offered his hand. "Thank you, Tommie. I'm delighted."

Tommie stared at him and then his hand. Finally she extended her own. "Yes, well, I—I'm happy for you. He will, of course, continue to show the house until the closing."

"I don't want strangers going through my house!" Pete protested.

"I'm afraid he has that right."

Pete turned to the receptionist. "Get Larry Miller at the bank on the line, please." Then he turned and headed down the hall. "I'll be back in a minute."

Tommie tried to pull herself together. She knew the best way to do so was to focus on her work. To that end she walked over to the women, who were talking to their husbands.

"Which one of you wants to go first tomorrow morning?" she asked, trying to set her schedule.

The youngest woman immediately volunteered. Then Patti and Adele requested the next day. They wanted time to think about their choices. Tommie was writing down their decisions when Pete returned.

"We're closing next Monday," he announced.

"That soon? Can they get the paperwork done by then?" Tommie asked.

"Yes. The money is ready and they're going to work overtime to have everything done. And I'm paying the builder a fee to keep him from showing the house."

"All right. So he's going to remove the lockbox?"

"Yes. And tonight we'll celebrate with dinner. I'll pick you up at seven."

Tommie stared at him again. The man was out of control. "I haven't—"

"Yes, you have to celebrate with me, Tommie." He bent over and kissed her cheek. "See you at seven."

Then he disappeared into the conference room.

"Well, it looks like our leader won't be a bachelor for long," one of the men said.

Tommie stared at him, not realizing he was talking about her. By the time she did, he had followed his boss into the conference room.

"Um, Pete is just celebrating. That's all," she said to the women, who were smiling at her.

"It looked like fun," Adele said.

"Yes," Tommie absentmindedly agreed. In her mind she was reliving the moment when he'd kissed her.

* * *

When Pete picked her up that evening, she greeted him with a wary smile. But he was well behaved.

"I hope you like Italian. I made a reservation at a restaurant I like."

"That's fine."

"Did you notice the keys on my key ring?"

She looked down at his keys in the ignition, but frowned, unable to determine his meaning. "What?"

"I have the new house key. I thought we'd go there after dinner."

"I understand you want to see it again, but you don't have to drag me along. It's your house now."

"I agree, but I need to talk to you about it." He pulled into the parking lot of the restaurant and parked the car.

Tommie didn't wait for him to come open her door. She didn't want him to think this was a date.

When they entered the restaurant, she realized she was in trouble. They were shown to an intimate booth with swinging doors that shut out the rest of the room. The table was covered with a red-checkered tablecloth, and several candles lent a warm glow to the space.

"This is...very nice," she said, avoiding his gaze.

"I can recommend the lasagne or the chicken alfredo," Pete said as she picked up the menu.

After a moment of silence while she hid behind the menu, the waiter arrived. She looked up and ordered, as did Pete.

"Would you like to share a bottle of wine?" he asked.

"Sorry. It gives me a headache."

Once the waiter moved away and the swinging doors closed, Pete leaned forward. "I've got an idea."

"About what?"

"The house. I didn't make much of a home in my condo in Boston. Just serviceable furniture that met my basic needs. I never entertained and to tell the truth I didn't spend much time at home myself. I was always at the office. Whatever I had I sold when I left. So basically I'm starting from scratch."

"Really? You sold everything?" Tommie couldn't believe he had lived like that. Now he had a wonderful house, the one she loved, and she hoped he'd make it a home.

"Yeah. None of it would look good here anyway."

"I see."

"That's where you come in."

"I beg your pardon? Me?"

The waiter chose that moment to bring their salads and drinks. Tommie waited impatiently for him to leave. As soon as he did, she asked, "What does this have to do with me?"

"I want you to furnish the house for me."

"I'm a Realtor not an interior decorator," she said firmly.

"I know that," Pete said as he picked up his fork. He took a bite of salad and chewed it while Tommie stared at him. "Eat your salad," he added.

Like a zombie, she picked up her fork. She chewed

slowly, thinking about what he'd said. But it didn't make sense. She didn't know his taste. Besides, there was no way she could furnish his house and still get her own work done.

"I realize I'd be asking a lot," he said, looking at her, "but I thought maybe your sisters could help."

She stared at him. "How could I possibly choose what you would have to live with? That's an impossible request!"

Instead of answering, he took another forkful of salad. Then he tore off a piece of bread. "Want some bread?"

"No, thank you." Finally she continued to her salad, deciding she'd convinced him how ludicrous his proposal was.

Just as she relaxed, he spoke again.

"I trust your taste. I want you to decorate the house as if it was yours. You loved the house, didn't you? I think that's what you said."

"Yes, I loved the house, but that doesn't mean— I don't have the time."

They continued eating, but Tommie was nervous. She sensed they hadn't finished their discussion. She tried not to think about what he'd asked. She did love that house, and she had pictured how she would decorate the place when she first saw it. But it wasn't hers. She had to remember that.

Besides, Tabitha was busy making her video. Teresa could help, and had great taste, but Tommie didn't want to ask her to give up her summer to do this favor for Pete.

"I'll give you ten thousand for the two weeks' worth of work."

She stared at him. "For that much money, you could hire a good decorator!"

"I don't want a decorator. I don't want my house to look like a show house. I want it to look like a home. Your place looked classy but comfortable. That's what I want."

She knew what he meant. She'd been in model homes. While they all made for pretty pictures, few of them exuded a sense of home.

She was going to make a lot in commission from selling the houses to his staff. But Teresa could use the money....

"I'll have to talk it over with Teresa," she said slowly, not sure that the two of them could even pull it off.

"Great! You'll need to get started Monday."

Tommie leaned back against the booth. "Wait! I didn't agree. I said I'd talk to Teresa."

"What about Tabitha?"

"She's busy making her videos."

The waiter pushed open the doors, his hands filled with their orders. "Was there something wrong with the salads?" he asked.

Tommie looked at her plate and realized she'd eaten very little. "No, not at all."

"Want me to bring these later?" the waiter asked, lifting the dishes to show he meant their entrées.

"No," Pete said. "We'll keep them. They'll be fine."

"I'll be right back to refill your glasses," the waiter assured them.

Pete nodded, frustration on his face. But he said nothing until after their glasses were filled and the waiter finally disappeared.

"The reason I want it all done in two weeks is that I'm going to give a party and have all my people over. Sort of a welcome-to-Texas party. I can't do that without furniture. And I don't have time to put the house together."

"Have you booked your mother's caterer?"

"Not yet. Do I have to do it this early?" he asked.

"A good caterer can be hard to line up. You need to call them as soon as possible." Tommie moved her salad to the side and began eating her chicken alfredo. After a moment of silence, she asked, "What's your favorite color?"

"Why?"

After sighing, she said, "I thought it would be an important thing to know *if* we do your house for you."

"Oh, sure. My favorite color is blue. But I like most colors. I don't want a lot of black in the house. I like it open and light, with a mixture of colors."

"All right."

"I'd want my bedroom kind of, uh, masculine, but the other rooms could be frilly, if that's what you want."

"I'm not big on frilly, Pete. Sorry."

"No problem. I'm not either. So, will you talk to Teresa tonight? Should I call the caterer tomorrow?"

"Wait. You're expecting me to buy china and everything for the kitchen, too?"

Pete nodded.

"All of that will be expensive."

He grinned. "My company has been doing well for a number of years. I have the money, Tommie. I've already set aside money to furnish the house." He named a six-digit figure.

Tommie shook her head.

"What's wrong? Is that not enough?"

"No, I think it's too much. For that kind of money you need a professional decorator. Not me."

Pete leaned forward and looked at her intently, reminding her of his kiss earlier that day. His voice took on a low, smooth tone as he said, "No, I need you."

With only a little imagination, she could believe he meant those words literally. The romantic cocoon created by the cozy table and the candlelight wrapped itself around her and drew her in. And she was going willingly. She felt herself leaning, her eyes lowering until—

She came to her senses and pulled back, the voice inside her head screaming, *He's not The One!*

"He wants what?" Teresa said with astonishment.

Tommie moved the phone a couple of inches from her ear until Teresa settled down. "He doesn't want a decorator because they don't create a home. They create a showcase. He's offering us a lot of money. You'd make ten thousand."

"And what will you make?" Teresa asked after a moment.

"Uh, the same."

"Tommie, you're lying, and you know you're a lousy liar. You're giving all the money to me."

"Well, you'd have to do most of the legwork, waiting at the house for deliveries. I thought—"

"You thought you'd take care of your baby sister again."

"But I'm making a lot of money selling these houses."

"Of course you are," Teresa countered. "It's your job."

"So you should take the money for the decorating." Why wouldn't her sister see reason? "After all, you're better at it than me. You helped me do my place."

"And I enjoyed it every minute."

Exasperated, Tommie let out a long sigh. "Well, then, how about I take ten percent? This way the person with the most talent takes the most money."

"Fifty-fifty."

"Eighty-twenty?"

"Fifty-fifty."

When had her sister become so hard-nosed? Tommie wondered. "Seventy-thirty—my last offer."

"You've got a deal."

Tommie put the key in the lock and opened the door to Pete's house the next morning.

As she entered, Teresa gasped. "Oh, it's beautiful! I should pay him for the privilege of decorating this house."

Tommie followed her into the foyer. "Now you see why I fell in love with this place the first time I saw it."

"Maybe that's why Pete asked you to furnish the house. Or it could be he's interested in more than just a decorator." Teresa smiled, but there was a question in her eyes.

"No, that's not it at all." But as Tommie walked her sister through the first floor, she couldn't help envisioning herself as the mistress of this gorgeous home. She saw the furnishings that would make it a home.

They mutually turned to the stairs and climbed them slowly, looking down on the splendor of the foyer and living room. The three secondary bedrooms were closest to the stairs, so Tommie led the way to those bedrooms, each of which had its own bath.

"Wouldn't we have enjoyed having our own bathrooms growing up?" Teresa whispered.

"Yes, it was a dream of mine, especially when Tabitha did her hair."

Teresa laughed softly. "She did take a long time, but it always looked good."

"Yes. Do you think we should do all three of these rooms with queen-size beds?"

"Maybe we should ask Pete if he wants one room with twin beds for any children."

"I doubt that. He doesn't have any children and neither does Jim."

"No. Neither of them is married, either."

Tommie thought about how two thirty-one-year-old men, both handsome and successful in their own right, had remained unhitched. "Did Jim express any interest in marriage?" she asked as she escorted her sister past the second bedroom.

"No, he didn't. At least not to me. I mean he didn't mention that subject to me." Teresa got all flustered, her cheeks turning red.

Tommie shifted her concerns from decorating to her sister's feelings. "Are you disappointed?"

"You're being silly," Teresa told her. "We haven't known each other very long."

"I guess you're right. Anyway," she said as she opened another door, "here's the pièce de résistance—the master bedroom." She said it with an air of a magician presenting an incredible trick.

The trick was on her when Pete sat up in a sleeping bag on the floor, his chest oh-so-bare.

Chapter Six

"What time is it?" Pete asked in a fuzzy voice.

Tommie didn't answer. She couldn't. She stood frozen, her gaze fastened on Pete's chest. Broad, muscular and naked. Had a man ever looked so beautiful?

"It's nine o'clock," Teresa said from beside her.

"Damn! I overslept!" Pete moved to get up, but then he stopped. "Uh, I need to get up…if you don't mind excusing me."

Did he mean he was totally naked under those covers? Tommie wondered silently. She never thought she'd see the day when she'd be jealous of a sleeping bag!

Clearing her throat, Teresa grabbed her arm, leading her to the door. "We'll be downstairs."

Tommie backpedaled out of the bedroom, her eyes never leaving Pete's chest. It was only when they closed the bedroom door behind them that she came to her senses. "What is he doing? He can't sleep on the floor."

Teresa chuckled. "I guess he can, Tommie, since he did."

"That's ridiculous! He's got a perfectly good bed at his mother's."

"Would you want to move back home with Mom? She still expects us to have a curfew."

"I know, but he's a man. Surely his mother—"

Teresa laughed again. "Yeah, you know she's like that, too."

"But he only had to wait two weeks."

"Well, I suspect he slept here because this is his first house. You said he was excited."

Tommie closed her eyes and remembered the kiss they'd exchanged when she'd given him the news. "Yes—yes, he was excited."

"Tell you what, I'll go to Starbucks and get us some coffee and pastries. I'll be right back." Teresa ran down the stairs and out the door before Tommie could think of a reason not to find breakfast for Pete Schofield.

She finally moved down the stairs into the kitchen area. Since there were no chairs in the house, they would have to eat breakfast standing. But, of course, she and Teresa had already eaten breakfast.

A while later, hearing footsteps on the stairs, she

moved to the foyer to intercept Pete. "Why did you sleep here?" she asked him in a raised voice.

He came to an abrupt halt. "It's my house, isn't it? So I can sleep wherever I damn well please!"

"But you have no furniture!"

"I know that!" He took a deep breath. "Why are we yelling at each other?"

"I just think you're behaving foolishly."

Pete sighed. "Look, Tommie, I appreciate your concern, but I'm fine, except that I overslept. Now, if you don't mind, I—"

Teresa pushed the front door open. "I'm not too late, am I?" She looked at Pete. "We thought you could use some coffee and a little breakfast."

"How thoughtful of you, Teresa," Pete said, using his charming smile.

"Shall we have your first meal in the kitchen?" Teresa suggested, smiling.

Pete gave a slight bow and waved her forward. "After you, Teresa…and Tommie."

Tommie followed her sister, irritated with both of them. It had been sweet of Teresa to think of breakfast for Pete. She would've thought of it if she hadn't been so surprised that he was sleeping on the floor of his new house. And so taken by the sight of his naked chest, she added.

"So, have you and Tommie agreed to furnish the house for me?" Pete asked.

Teresa looked at her sister. "Tommie, do you want to answer that question?"

"Yes, we've agreed. But we'll need to work out how much we have to spend and how we handle the money," Tommie said stiffly.

"I've already told you what I set aside. As for how to handle it, I'll open an account in your name and put the money in there. That will work, won't it?" Pete asked, his voice casual.

Tommie stared at him. "That's a lot of money."

"It's a big house. And if you need more, let me know. I'll have a checkbook for you this afternoon."

Tommie swallowed. Then she stiffened her shoulders. "We'll try to furnish the master bedroom first, so you won't have to sleep on the floor too long."

"That would be greatly appreciated," he said with a grin. "Now, I've got to go. I'll take my coffee with me. And thanks a lot."

He headed for the back door that opened into the garage.

"This is going to be fun," Teresa said, letting her gaze roam the room. "We'll get to choose even the china. Oh, I'm going to love this!"

"Actually, I am, too. I think he's crazy, but that's not my fault. Can we start shopping tonight? I should be finished by four."

"Great. Pick me up then. I'll start making a list of what all we have to buy. And it's going to be a long one."

Tommie's day was going well. She'd gotten signed contracts on two more houses, and the two new couples looked at several houses before the day was done. They would go out again in the morning.

At four, she was clearing her desk so she could pick up Teresa. She'd called her sister to let her know she was running a little late.

"Ah, here you are," Pete said as he entered the office. "I was afraid I'd miss you."

"Do you need something?"

"I wanted to give you the checkbook and bank card. I thought you might be starting this evening."

"Yes, we are."

"Do you know what you're going to buy?"

"Tonight? Probably things for your bedroom. Teresa has made a huge list of what we have to purchase. I'll show it to you tomorrow so you can cross out anything you don't want us to buy."

"Are you picking her up now?"

"Yes."

He hesitated. Then he said, "Why don't I go with you this evening. I can look at the list while we have dinner."

"I really don't think— I mean, we'll be covering a lot of territory this evening."

"I can keep up. Come on, Tommie. It'll be fun."

What could she say? It was his house, his money and soon to be his furniture. "Of course."

Since he followed her in his car, she was able to call Teresa and warn her.

"That will be fine, Tommie. I imagine he's eager to get started."

Tommie was glad her sister could take the change in their plans so easily. She herself felt unsettled. Was it because she didn't want Pete to realize how good Teresa was at decorating? That he would think less of her because she didn't have talent in that area? Why would it matter what he thought?

Fortunately, she didn't have to answer that question, because they reached Teresa's house. Pete insisted they use his car, so Teresa got in the back, insisting her sister take the front passenger seat.

They went to one of the nicer department stores. On the way, Teresa first read the list for Pete's bedroom and bath.

"I think you've thought of everything, Teresa. That list sounds good. And I definitely want a king-size bed."

"Of course. We thought we could get a lot of things at the department store. They carry high-quality merchandise, and with everything in the same store, it would be faster."

"Good thinking."

Tommie added, "About your bedroom, we're going to look for a comforter and draperies with blue as the basic color and take accent colors from the print of the comforter."

The first department they visited was furniture. But Pete didn't find any bedroom set he liked. He did purchase a mattress and box spring he wanted in king-size. Then he negotiated delivery on Monday, when he would actually have signed the papers. Tommie arranged for other purchases to be delivered at the same time.

Then they purchased sheets, pillows and found a comforter that satisfied all of them. It was dark blue with primary colors running through it.

Tommie found big, fluffy towels that matched the colors exactly.

"Tommie, here are the peach ones we wanted," Teresa called out.

"Peach? I don't really want peach," Pete said, frowning.

"Not for your bathroom. These would be for the guest bathroom on the first floor. We thought it would be a good idea to pick a different color for each of the bathrooms. That would make it easy for whoever does the laundry."

"Good idea."

When they had all the towels picked out, Tommie asked that they be sent to the furniture department to be delivered with the bed. Then she took four towel sets out of the navy stack. "These we want to take with us."

"Why?" Pete asked as the saleswoman put those in a shopping bag.

"So you could start using them at once."

Next they moved to the appliance department and bought a washer and dryer. After that purchase, Pete suggested they go eat. Jim, whom he'd called earlier and asked to meet them, was joining them at the restaurant.

Teresa exclaimed, "How nice."

Tommie noticed the flush in her sister's cheeks. She didn't think Pete did, however.

When they reached the restaurant, Jim was already there. He stood as they reached the table and pulled out Teresa's chair. Pete did the same for Tommie.

Once they'd ordered, Pete began telling his brother of their purchases.

"On one hand, Mom will be greatly relieved since she hated you living in your house without any furniture. On the other hand, she's going to be hurt that she wasn't asked to furnish the house for you."

"So you shouldn't tell her," Pete said crisply.

"Pete! She'll have to know soon."

"I'll tell her I bought the house already furnished."

The other three laughed. Jim protested, "Even Mom wouldn't believe that lie."

"I'll think of something to say."

"She could come shopping with us a few times, Pete," Teresa said.

Tommie closed her eyes. Did her sister not remember Mrs. Schofield? Instead, she said, "I suppose we could invite her to join us once or twice."

"I don't think she'd last much longer than that," Jim said. "Her idea of shopping is to sit on a sofa and have the salesladies bring out things she might like."

"There's no need to do that," Pete told them. "She'd only slow you down."

Tommie was enormously grateful for the reprieve, and she avoided the topic for the remainder of dinner.

When they had finished, she suggested they return to the department store to buy things for the kitchen. "We could buy a coffeemaker for you."

"Are they hard to operate?" Pete asked.

Tommie and Teresa stared at him.

"You've never used one before?" Tommie asked.

"I lived near a Starbucks in Boston. I dropped in there on the way to the office."

Jim grinned. "He's not used to doing for himself."

"It's easy," Tommie said. "Even I can do it."

Friday, Pete called Tommie first thing in the morning. "You busy tonight?"

"I beg your pardon?"

"This is Pete. Are you busy tonight?"

"Yes, actually, I am." Even if she hadn't had plans, she would've told him she did. She was beginning to think he counted her as his personal assistant.

"Oh. Is it anything you can cancel?"

"No, it's not."

There was a long silence. Then he said, "How about Saturday night?"

"What is it you want, Pete?"

"I thought I'd give a party for everyone at the restaurant we had dinner at the other night. They have a private room in the back. Could you come Saturday night?"

"Yes, I suppose I could, but—"

"Okay, I'll let you know what time."

And he hung up the phone.

Tommie stared at the receiver. Then she gently put it in its place. The man was insane. She'd shown him how to make coffee, and she'd brought over the clean towels for him. They'd bought some elegant coffee mugs, and Teresa had spent several days lining the cabinets.

In addition, she and Teresa had made several more shopping expeditions, crossing off things on Teresa's list. Tommie knew Pete was busy getting his company operational, but it seemed to her that he'd absolved himself of any effort to create a home.

So she was creating the house she would want. The only problem would be walking away from it once she and Teresa had finished.

The phone rang again and Tommie assumed a professional air. "Good morning, this is Tommie Tyler. May I help you?"

"Yes, you may."

Tommie recognized Mrs. Schofield's voice, and she didn't sound happy.

"Mrs. Schofield, how nice to hear from you."

"Yes, dear, but Jim told me you're helping Pete furnish his home. I don't understand why he didn't ask me."

"I think he was concerned about the stress it would cause you, Mrs. Schofield. He needs the home completed in another week, for a party he's giving. Did he ask you for the name of your caterer? He said you would know how to arrange things."

"He did ask for their name and number."

Tommie thought she sounded disappointed. Though she knew the woman would slow them down, she and Teresa had planned to shop tonight for the china and crystal. "I was going to call you today, but I didn't want to call too early. My sister and I are shopping for the china and crystal. We would certainly appreciate your coming with us. After all, you have much more experience at entertaining than we do."

"Oh, I'd love to. What time shall we meet?"

After they made arrangements, Tommie hung up the phone with a sigh. They might spend more money than she'd planned this evening, but she'd made his mother feel better. That was important. Which reminded her she needed to call her mother.

Pete came out of a meeting and checked his watch. It was almost noon. He wondered if he could catch Tommie for lunch. He wanted to know with whom she was spending the evening.

He'd been taken aback by her brisk refusal of his invitation for tonight. He guessed he'd taken her for granted. But he had so much to do to get set up here. His business, at this stage, was more important than his house. But he'd admit he couldn't wait until Monday when things started arriving. If for no other reason because he was tired of sleeping on the floor. It made him feel old when he woke up every morning.

When someone else answered Tommie's phone, he

knew he wasn't going to see her at lunch. He left a message for her to call him. In the meantime, he couldn't help thinking about her out with another man.

"Mr. Schofield, you have a call on line three," the receptionist said.

Normally, his secretary screened his calls, but he took the phone. "Hello?"

"Darling, it's your mother."

"Hi, Mom, how are you doing?"

"Fine. I'm going to pick out your china tonight."

Pete had been leaning against the desk. At her words, he stiffened and stood up straight. "What?"

"Well, that darling girl you brought to meet me asked me to accompany her and her sister on a shopping trip. She realized how much experience I've had entertaining. And she explained why you didn't ask me to furnish the house. That was so thoughtful of you."

He made a mental note to thank Tommie for saving his hide. "I'm glad you think so. When did you say you're going shopping?"

"This evening. It's fortunate I didn't already have plans. But I'm delighted to contribute to your new home."

"I know that, Mom. Just be sure you don't overdo it."

"That's exactly what Jim said. I'm so lucky to have such devoted sons."

"Okay, I've got to go, Mom."

After he hung up the phone, he hurried to his office. Tommie had made it sound as if she had a date tonight.

Instead, she was escorting his mother on a shopping trip.

One of his men stuck his head in the door. "Pete? Some of us are going to Joe T. Garcia's. Want to join us?"

"I thought you usually joined your wife," Pete said.

· "Not today. Tommie's taking all the ladies to lunch. Did you forget?"

Pete pretended to have forgotten what he'd never known. "Oh, yeah, that's right. Sure, I'll join you. I haven't been to Joe T.'s since I got back."

"I just wanted to tell you how much we appreciate Tommie's efforts. My wife is feeling right at home here. Fort Worth is a friendly town, but Tommie, in particular, has made them all feel welcome. They actually are unhappy to go back home on Monday."

"Which just means we'll get to welcome them again," Pete assured him, walking with him toward the front door.

He reminded himself to thank Tommie when he talked to her. Right after he chastised her for misleading him.

Dressed to the nines, Evelyn Schofield was sitting on a velvet chair at an antique desk usually reserved for brides. She had the undivided attention of the salesclerk.

As soon as Tommie and Teresa entered the china department, the woman spotted them.

"Oh, my darling girls," she cooed. "I'm so excited about our task this evening." She ushered them close.

"I've been discussing our choices with this lovely lady. What is your name, dear?"

"Nelda Bloom, ma'am."

"Isn't that just a perfect name for someone in the bridal department?"

Tommie and Teresa exchanged a worried look. "Thank you for helping us, Ms. Bloom. We'd like a pattern that's up-to-date, preferably with blue trim."

"Mrs. Schofield already requested something blue. She said it's her son's favorite color." The clerk smiled at Pete's mother.

"I've gone ahead and preselected several patterns from different companies, all top-of-the-line, of course."

Tommie knew which one she liked at once. The delicate beauty of the china was enhanced with blue flowers, exquisitely wrought around the edges. She held her tongue, allowing Mrs. Schofield to look at the patterns.

"I need to see the cups of these three patterns," Mrs. Schofield ordered crisply.

Tommie breathed a sigh of relief that her favorite was included in the three. "We thought service for twelve, Mrs. Schofield. Do you think that's too much?"

"Oh, no, child, not at all. You should order service for twenty-four."

The salesclerk's eyes practically lit up. No doubt she worked on a commission.

Tommie reached out her left hand to pick up the delicate cup of the pattern she liked. "This is really lovely," she said as she held it up to Mrs. Schofield.

"Oh!" Mrs. Schofield shrieked. "How terrible!"

Chapter Seven

The shrill cry startled Tommie and she almost dropped the cup. Once she had it under control, she looked at Mrs. Schofield. "You don't like this pattern?"

"Oh, it's a lovely pattern, my dear. If you like it, then I think we should choose it." She leaned closer to Tommie and lowered her voice to a conspiratorial whisper. "But I want to apologize for my son. I know he's busy, but he shouldn't be sending you out to choose the china without him. Especially since he hasn't gotten you a ring yet!"

"A ring?" Tommie asked, confused by the turn of the conversation. Mrs. Schofield reached out and grabbed her left hand, as if trying to hide her son's faux pas. Then the meaning hit Tommie. "Oh, no! Mrs. Schofield,

I'm working for your son. There's nothing personal about it. He's paying us."

The older woman yanked her hand back. "I see. Well…even if it started out that way, surely you can't resist him. He is very handsome, you know."

"I—I certainly agree that he's attractive, but I can assure you we're just business associates. Nothing more." Tommie hoped she'd convinced the woman.

"Well, I think you would make a perfect bride. I'll speak to him about it as soon as I see him."

"Oh, no! No, don't do that. We need to concentrate on choosing the china. I really like this pattern. Don't you?"

"Oh, yes. It's lovely. Teresa, dear, do you think so?"

"Yes, I do. But what crystal pattern do you think goes with it?"

That question got both the salesclerk's and Mrs. Schofield's attention. Tommie nodded a thank-you to Teresa. Her plan of including Mrs. Schofield was backfiring on her.

Both Teresa and Tommie worked hard to keep the subject on what Pete needed in his house. His mother chose a number of silver trays, a bar set and several other items after they had decided on the crystal. Twenty-four of every size and shape went down on the order pad.

Tommie explained that all the purchases should be sent to the furniture department so it could be delivered on Monday morning.

"Oh, that's good planning, Tommie. Now, does he

have a dining-room set? I know a wonderful store nearby. Shall I show you?"

"First let me show you some breakfast stools for the kitchen. I saw them here the other day. There's a nice breakfast bar in the house where Pete could have his coffee. Right now he has no place to sit."

"Oh, mercy, I didn't realize he was roughing it so much," his mother said and rose to follow Tommie.

Tommie bit her cheek to keep from laughing. It was hard to call living in that house roughing it, even if there was no furniture.

Mrs. Schofield approved of the stools and Tommie ordered four to be delivered on Monday. Before they left, Mrs. Schofield suggested they stroll through the furniture department. Within an hour, they had furnished the dining room, the master bedroom and a second bedroom. Plus, Tommie had selected a beautiful antique desk for Pete's study, and a leather chair that looked terrific with it.

"I think we'd better call it a night," Tommie told Mrs. Schofield. "You've been a wonderful help. We wouldn't have gotten nearly as much done without you."

"I need to meet your mother, Tommie. She has raised such charming daughters. I don't know how she managed on her own."

Teresa smiled. "She's a strong woman, Mrs. Schofield. We'll invite you both to lunch once we've finished furnishing Pete's house. That would be fun."

"Yes, it certainly would. Well, I've enjoyed myself.

I'll have to tell Pete what a good job you're doing." With a wave goodbye, Mrs. Schofield was off.

As soon as they were in her car, Tommie let out an audible breath. "Whew! I hope she doesn't talk to Pete anytime soon."

"She probably won't. I think he's staying pretty busy. I talked to Jim last night and he was complaining he had hardly seen Pete since he'd come home."

"He's extra busy right now. I'm sure he'll have more time for Jim and his mother once he gets the company back on schedule again."

"You're defending him?" Teresa asked, a sly smile on her lips.

"No, I just— Teresa! You were teasing me."

"I just wanted to know how you felt about him."

"He's a nice man. That's all. I've told you before I'm not interested in having children two or three at a time. And I'm not a stay-at-home-mom type like you. I have a career."

"Those things can be worked out, you know."

"Maybe, if both people want to work it out. That's not the case here."

"Okay." Teresa got out of the car and then bent over to look at her sister. "Just be sure before you burn your bridges."

Tommie waved goodbye and drove home. It was late and she was tired. She pulled in to the garage attached to her condo. Then she entered her home, switching on lights as she went.

A knock on the front door surprised her. She couldn't imagine who would be at her door at ten o'clock at night. She advanced cautiously and looked through the peephole.

Then she backed away. "What do you want, Pete?"

"I want to talk to you."

"Look, I tried to explain to your mother. I guess she didn't listen carefully. There's nothing to worry about."

"Open the door, Tommie! I refuse to carry on a conversation through the door."

Reluctantly she undid the locks on the door and opened it, but not wide enough for him to enter.

"I want to come in, Tommie."

"It's late."

"I won't stay long."

She finally allowed him to enter. "I explained to your mother, Pete. It's not my fault if she didn't understand."

"What did you explain to my mother?"

"That we're not—" She stopped before she said too much. He obviously had no idea about Mrs. Schofield's intention that they marry. "Did you talk to your mother?"

Pete grinned. "No, but I'm dying to know what you had to explain to her."

"Never mind. It doesn't matter." She looked away and refused to meet his gaze. "I'm tired."

"What did you explain to my mother?"

"It doesn't matter. More importantly, we bought a lot tonight. And it will all be delivered Monday morning."

"You'll be there for the delivery?"

"Yes, I will."

"So, do you need more money?"

Tommie's eyes widened. "Not at all, even though your mother insisted you needed service for twenty-four."

"Okay. By the way, it wasn't very nice to mislead me the way you did."

Tommie took a step back. "What are you talking about?"

"Tonight. You made it sound like you had a date." He moved closer to her.

"I did not. I said I had plans and that was exactly true. Besides, if I'd had a date, it's none of your business."

He cocked one eyebrow at her, but then he changed the subject. "My men want me to tell you how much they appreciate the way you've made their wives feel at home here."

Tommie breathed a sigh of relief that the conversation had turned to business rather than personal matters. "They're very nice women and I've enjoyed myself."

"Good."

She expected him to take his leave then, but he continued to stand there, smiling, as if he expected something more.

"Was there something else?" she finally asked.

"I guess not. I haven't had much time for—for a social life, so I've missed getting to know you."

Tommie frowned. "I'm working for you, Pete. Remember? You're paying me for what I'm doing. You don't owe me any 'personal' time." She took another step back.

His eyes narrowed. "You seem nervous."

"I am. We don't fit together, Pete. I'm a career woman, and I don't want to have two or three babies at once. You're an old-fashioned guy who wants his woman in the kitchen. It would be a big mistake for us to get too close."

"It felt pretty good the other day when I kissed you," he said softly.

"Marriage shouldn't be based on feeling good. You're an attractive man. I'll admit I was drawn to you at first, but I've realized we wouldn't make each other happy. So let's keep our distance."

"What if I don't want to?"

"So you're telling me you don't mind having a wife who has a demanding career?"

"Well, no, but you could change," he suggested, smiling.

"Not if that's not what I want."

"How do you know what you want if you keep your distance?"

"Because I'm using my head."

He reached out and took her by the shoulders, pulling her closer. "Well, I don't think I'm using my head, but I can't get that kiss out of my mind. I need to kiss you again so I'll know if it was the excitement of getting the house or you that made it hard to focus the rest of the day."

Tommie felt her cheeks flush. "I'm sure it was the house."

He moved closer to her. "I'm not so sure. I'm not thinking about the house now. All I can think about are your lips."

"Pete—"

He stopped her protest with his lips. They closed over hers as his arms wrapped around her, holding her against him. She could feel his strength, his heat, as his lips molded to hers in a soul-searching kiss. Even her thoughts of protest disappeared like mist and her heart raced.

When he finally pulled back slightly, she drew a deep breath, trying to regain control. Before that happened, he kissed her again, raising the heat factor. His hands moved up and down her back, pressing her more tightly against him, but she needed no encouragement. To the dismay of the small part of her brain that remained sane, she was more than cooperating with Pete's plan.

Pete was overwhelmed by his response to Tommie. She drove him crazy with wanting more. His hands shifted to her firm bottom and he wanted to throw her over his shoulder and find the nearest bed. He deepened his kiss even more, then broke it off to whisper her name. He trailed kisses down her neck before he returned to her lips.

"Pete, we mustn't—"

He cut her off. He didn't want to stop. Didn't want

her to explain again how they weren't suited for each other. His body was telling him differently. He'd never experienced the magic that pervaded him now. It was overwhelming.

Tommie forced herself out of his arms and backed away. "Pete, we can't do this. I won't do this!"

"You're saying no?" His voice was incredulous. She'd felt so right in his arms, so...perfect, he found her behavior hard to conceive.

"You know I'm not what you want."

"It didn't feel that way." His gaze was focused on her slightly swollen lips. Hunger surged through him again.

"You're not thinking, Pete. You'd be unhappy with me. I don't cook. I don't stay home. I don't want a houseful of kids all born on the same day. Could you live with those things?"

He paused to think about it, but she didn't wait for an answer.

"You couldn't! You've already told me what you want, and it's not me. So my response to our...kissing is no, stop."

She was emphasizing that a little too much in his opinion. "Fine, I got the message. You don't have to keep saying no."

Anger was building in him that she didn't feel what he felt. The miracle of their fitting so well together hadn't touched her.

"Go home, Pete," Tommie said with exhaustion in her voice.

"I'm going. And I'll *try* to keep myself under control around you from now on," he told her, sarcasm heavy in his voice.

He walked out and slammed the door behind him. Then he felt bad about his response. It hadn't been the most mature moment in his life. But her response had hurt. For the first time, he'd felt the magic all the songs and books talked about. He hadn't even believed in its existence before tonight.

And she'd rejected him.

Was she right? Was a union between them a mistake?

Could he compromise on what he thought his wife should be? Could she? He couldn't expect her to do all the changing. She'd made that clear.

He was surprised when he discovered he'd reached his house. His mind had been on the last few minutes at Tommie's, not on his driving.

Pulling in to the garage, he turned off his car, closed the garage door and entered his beautiful, empty house.

Wishing Tommie was in it.

All three sisters were going to the party Saturday night. Brett had asked Tabitha, Jim, Teresa and, of course, Pete, Tommie. Tommie was the only one who drove herself to the party. She'd refused Pete's stilted offer when he'd called Saturday morning.

She'd worked all day in the office, taking phone calls and reviewing her files. Anything to keep her mind off

Pete. She hadn't been totally honest with him last night. She hadn't wanted to say no. The feeling that had surged through her had overridden her caution and had frightened her.

Avoiding Pete was the smartest thing she could do. Hence she was driving herself to the party. She intended to mingle with her new friends and elude Pete at every turn.

Which didn't explain the sexy red dress she chose to wear. She had the right to look good without planning a seduction. Wearing sackcloth and ashes wasn't required.

She sucked in a deep breath before she entered the restaurant. *Sanity* was the word for the night, she reminded herself. She'd intentionally arrived late so there would be no awkward moments alone with Pete.

She needn't have worried. Pete was flirting with a very attractive waitress when Tommie entered. Since he saw her out of the corner of his eye and turned back to the waitress, Tommie realized he was trying to send her a message. He had no more interest in her.

Fine. That was what she wanted, wasn't it?

Greeting the wives and asking about their plans, in addition to greeting her sisters, carried Tommie through the before-dinner time. When everyone began to take their seats, Tommie approached with trepidation the vacant chair where Pete stood waiting.

"It's not the electric chair, Tommie," Pete muttered in her ear as he pushed in her seat.

Okay, so he'd noticed her lack of enthusiasm. She'd have to do better than that.

"Thank you, Pete. Did you have a good day?"

"Better than you. I wasn't working."

"You had to work today?" Adele asked. She was sitting on the other side of Pete.

"Yes, I did. Saturdays are big days for Realtors."

"Then you wouldn't be a good soccer mom. Saturdays are big days for soccer games," Adele said with a rueful smile.

"I've heard that. So both your kids are into soccer?"

"And everything else. They lead busier lives than I do. I'm just the chauffeur."

Tommie avoided looking at Pete. "Maybe you'll find better ways to occupy yourself when you get settled here. Car pools are good alternatives."

"True. And with all of us living in the same neighborhood, it will be convenient," Adele pointed out.

"Good planning on Pete's part," Tommie added.

"Thanks," Pete muttered. "Glad I'm good for something."

"Pete, are you upset?" Adele asked.

Her question came at a lull in the conversation, and the entire room stared at Pete.

"Boss? Something wrong?" one of the men asked.

Bill leaned over and whispered something in Adele's ear, and she shook her head.

Pete finally responded. "Nothing's wrong. In fact, after I visited with several influential men yesterday, I meant to tell you things are looking pretty good. We may need to start interviewing more people to keep up with the demand."

His words brought smiles to everyone's faces. Except for Tommie's. She knew he was irritated with her, and that had caused Adele's comment. She'd felt sure he'd complain to her before the night was over.

Under her breath, Adele muttered, "Sorry."

"No big deal," Pete whispered in return.

There was an awkward silence between the three of them, but Tommie didn't try to break it. What could she say? The man wanted sex and was unhappy that she'd said no? She didn't want to open their private lives to everyone in his company.

The waitresses began serving the entrée, and conversation broke off. When the redheaded waitress Pete had been talking to brought his plate, she gave him a big smile and leaned down to give him a glimpse of cleavage.

Several of the men around Pete and Tommie made a few suggestive remarks after the waitress disappeared into the kitchen. Tommie tried to look as if she was entranced with her steak.

"Sorry," Pete muttered.

"It's none of my business if you find her attractive."

"I'm not the only one."

"I never said you were."

"Come on, Tommie, quit acting like we're strangers!"

Tommie raised her gaze to his, determined to convince him that's exactly what they were.

She failed miserably and hurriedly looked away.

"I've been thinking," he said softly. "Maybe we could work things out."

She ignored him, putting butter on her baked potato.

"I could change," he murmured.

She needed him to back off. "Until you got in my pants, you mean?" she asked, using that inelegant expression to stop him in his tracks.

He gave her a hard look. "I don't like having my honesty impugned."

Ignoring him, she began eating her meal.

"We'll talk later," he snapped and addressed his meal also.

She didn't argue with his statement. But she prepared her response while other people were still around. She was *not* going to be alone with Pete again.

When the first couple excused themselves, after the meal had ended, Tommie stood and started to follow them out. Immediately Pete caught her arm and whispered, "If you leave now, everyone will know why I'm upset."

A debate raged in Tommie's head. If she stayed she might be tempted again, but if she left Pete's employees, her new friends would think she was being difficult.

At least here there would be people around to keep him in line. Perhaps that was the better choice. Besides, there wasn't anything he could say that would make a difference. Was there?

Tommie sighed. It was that nagging doubt that worried her. She definitely didn't want him to touch her again. She pulled her arm away and resumed her seat. She turned to speak to the man on her left, Brett, and Tabitha.

Still, Tommie was completely aware of Pete's every movement. And the redheaded waitress's arrival with a coffeepot to refill Pete's cup. The fact that she ignored the other empty cups around her and stood chatting with Pete was duly noted by Tommie.

Good thing she wasn't jealous, she assured herself. She didn't want to have any personal relationship with Pete. That was why she didn't get upset about the woman's blatant flirtation.

Of course she didn't.

"Could I have some coffee, or is it all reserved for Pete?" she asked with a knowing smile, when she really didn't even want any more.

"Yeah, me, too," Brett added.

"Oh, of course," the waitress agreed, sending a superior smile Tommie's way. She refilled her cup and then Brett's. "Anyone else?"

Several people around the table requested more and she reluctantly moved away from Pete.

Pete slid his arm around Tommie. "Thanks, honey. I thought she was going to crawl into my lap."

Then he leaned over and kissed Tommie.

So much for keeping things impersonal.

Chapter Eight

Tommie picked up Teresa early Monday. They were both excited about so many of their purchases arriving that morning.

"I went through our master list yesterday afternoon to see what we still needed to buy. I thought we had most of it done until I did that." Teresa had the list in her hands.

"Well, we may have a long way to go, but at least this morning we're going to see how much progress we've made."

"It's exciting, isn't it?" Teresa asked.

"Yes, it is. And I want to see Pete's face when he comes home to find a bed to sleep in. I can't believe he's been sleeping on the floor for so long."

"Me neither. Jim says he doesn't like roughing it."

"Well, at least we have that in common," Tommie said with a laugh. Then she looked at her sister. "You seem to be seeing Jim a lot. Are you falling for him?"

Teresa shook her head. "I think I'm just a convenient date for his brother's events."

"Oh. I'm sorry."

"Don't worry about it. I'm not heartbroken. Oh, let's drive through the Starbucks for coffee and a pastry this morning. I think we have plenty of time."

"Okay," Tommie agreed.

A few minutes later, armed with caffeine and sugar, they pulled up in front of the house. Tommie had managed to get her key in the lock, but before she could turn it, the door swung open.

"Who—Pete! What are you doing here?"

"I took the day off so I could see what you're doing. 'Morning, Teresa. Come on in."

"You didn't let me know you were going to be home." Tommie knew she sounded irritated, but she didn't like being surprised. Not after that morning she'd found him half-naked in the sleeping bag. She shivered at the thought.

"Sorry we don't have any coffee for you, Pete," Teresa said.

"It's all right. Remember Tommie bought me a coffeemaker. I've already got a full pot ready."

"Oh, good, because I need two cups to be fully functional in the morning," Teresa said with a smile. "And Tommie needs three."

Tommie frowned at her sister but said nothing. She walked into the kitchen and put her purse down on the counter. "I hope the delivery comes early. We need the washer and dryer connected at once.

"Why?" Pete asked, following her into the kitchen.

"We need to wash your sheets and dry them before we can put them on your bed."

"Aren't they clean?"

She turned to stare at him. "They'll feel better after they've been washed."

"Did you see all the work I've done?" Teresa asked. She opened a cabinet door so he could see the paper she'd used to line the shelves.

"That's nice. Did you—"

The ringing of the doorbell jolted them all and they surged toward the front door.

When Pete opened it, a man stood there. "Delivery for this address. You're expecting us, yes?"

"Yes, we are. Go right ahead and get started." Tommie indicated the way and stepped back.

He turned around and waved to several men standing on the sidewalk. They immediately went to the rear of the huge truck and began unloading boxes and packages.

"I guess we bought a lot," Tommie said with a shaky voice.

"You won't hear me complaining if it gets me off the floor."

Teresa laughed. "That's guaranteed, Pete. I think your room is the only one we've completely finished."

"Good."

Two hours later Pete was still pleased. The washer and dryer were connected, and his sheets and pillowcases were being dried. The master bedroom sported a king-size bed that was definitely masculine. Teresa and Tommie were hanging the curtains that matched the bedcovers.

He came into the room in time to lend a hand for the last curtain rod. "Man, I like this. I was afraid you'd come up with something all frilly."

Tommie rolled her eyes. "You said you didn't want frilly."

"Yeah, but what happens when I get married? My wife will want something different, won't she?"

"Maybe not. A vase of flowers and some art on the walls will make the room look more feminine."

"Good. By the way, I like those stools that you bought for the kitchen. And the dining room is beautiful."

"Your mother picked out most of the dining room."

"I thought they'd finished bringing things in, but the man in charge indicated they had some more. Do you know what it is?"

"I would guess it's some things I picked out for your office."

"You've finished my office?"

"No, I haven't come close to finishing it, but I've at least gotten started. Oh, and there's another bedroom set they're bringing up."

"There are boxes in the kitchen that haven't been opened," Pete pointed out.

"We haven't had time yet. We bought pots and pans, china and crystal, and everyday things. We'll get to them. I'm taking the entire day off." Tommie gave the curtain a final twitch and stood back to examine her work. "That doesn't look half-bad, does it?"

"It looks really good. Are the sheets done yet?"

"I'll go check," Tommie said hurriedly, ready to escape Pete's presence.

He followed her out of the room. "I want to see what you bought for my office."

Tommie said nothing. She knew he'd like the antique desk, but she didn't know how she knew. Maybe it was wishful thinking, because she really didn't know him that well.

They parted at the bottom of the stairs. She headed for the laundry room off the kitchen, and he went in the other direction toward his office.

Teresa stepped into the kitchen. "Shall I start unpacking these boxes?"

"Yes, that'd be great," Tommie called over her shoulder.

"Pete seems pleased."

"Of course he does. He hasn't done any work!"

"Tommie, you sound upset. Did he say something to irritate you?" Teresa asked.

"No, I'm sorry. I thought today would be so much fun, but he makes me nervous." She got the sheets and pillowcases out of the dryer and carried them upstairs. After she made the bed, she put on the new coverlet. Then she arranged the pillows she'd bought.

After backing away, she decided she'd done a good job. Then she wondered why she hadn't heard anything from Pete. Had he hated the antique desk? She headed down the stairs to his office.

When she reached the door, she stopped and stared. Pete was sitting behind the big desk, rubbing it with his hands.

"Do you like it?" she asked.

"It's perfect, honey. How did you know?"

She shrugged her shoulders. "Just a guess."

He got up and came around the desk. "You're a good guesser," he said softly and took her by her shoulders. Before she realized what he intended, he was kissing her...and she was enjoying it.

"Tommie— Oh!" Teresa broke off as she almost bumped into the couple.

Tommie pushed herself out of Pete's arms. "He—he liked the desk."

"Good. That's good. I had a question about the kitchen if you have a minute." Teresa backed away.

"Yes, of course," Tommie said, following her, leaving Pete standing at the door of his office.

"Sorry," Teresa whispered. "I didn't mean to interrupt."

"I'm glad you did. He's...tempting, but he's not what I want in a husband."

"What's wrong with him? He's obviously a good provider and a nice man."

"Yes, he is, but he doesn't want what I want."

"What do you want?"

"I want to be a success, to be able to provide for my family, to make sure they have everything they need," Tommie said, raising her chin as if she expected a challenge.

Teresa touched her sister's arm. "Tommie, we're all okay. You don't have to take care of us. Tabitha is going to do well with her videos, and I'm happy as a kindergarten teacher."

"Something could happen. It's best to be prepared."

"Tommie, you've got to take care of yourself. We'll be okay." Teresa put her arm around her sister's shoulder. "We don't want you to give up your happiness for us."

"I'm not! I'm doing what I want. I want to be a success, the top in my field. You know that."

"Couldn't you do that and maybe have a family, too?"

Tommie turned away from her sister. "No, I don't think so. Remember how tired Mom got trying to raise the three of us and hold down a full-time job? How we scraped by?"

"I remember a house filled with love. I remember a big sister who tried to take care of us even though she was only two minutes older than Tabitha. I remember learning to do things on my own and the pride I felt. It's better that everything isn't provided, Tommie. The parents who come into my class hovering over their children, making every decision for them, ruin their kids. They don't let them grow up, become self-sufficient."

Tommie turned back to her sister and hugged her. "I guess we all grew up self-sufficient, didn't we?"

"Mom did her best."

"Of course she did. But sometimes I wished—"

"Ladies?" Pete called.

Tommie turned her back and wiped her eyes so there was no suspicious moisture.

"Oh, here you are!" Pete exclaimed. "Jim just called. He said he'd pick up lunch for all of us and bring it over. He wants to see how things are going here."

"That's very nice of him," Teresa said with a smile. "I was beginning to get hungry. Oh, I forgot to tell you both that I ordered a breakfast table and chairs from Williams-Sonoma," she said, naming one of the premier housewares stores. "I found the furniture Saturday. It was on sale and I thought it was perfect for the breakfast nook. Maybe the delivery will get here before Jim."

"If it doesn't, we can eat at the breakfast bar, since we have the stools," Tommie said.

"I'll get out some plates." Teresa smiled at Pete. "It will be your first meal in your new house."

"Do we have dishes?" Pete asked.

Teresa opened the cabinets and showed him the everyday dishes they'd chosen and the glassware that went with it. "We have plenty of ice, too, in your refrigerator."

"Wow! I think I need to go grocery shopping to stock my pantry now. I can eat here instead of takeout or at a restaurant every evening. That's terrific."

Tommie said nothing.

"While I'm getting ready here, why don't you show Pete the bedroom since you've finished it," Teresa suggested.

"You're finished?" Pete asked.

"I had almost finished it when you were up there earlier. I just made the bed. That's the only part you haven't seen. Oh, and I put the towels and things in the bath."

"I'd like to see the finished product. Come on, Tommie, show me."

Tommie shot her sister a hard look. Then she led the way out of the kitchen to the stairway. Once they reached the bedroom, she paused in the doorway and motioned Pete to precede her into the room.

Pete did so willingly, and his gaze roamed the large bedroom. "Wow, this looks terrific." He crossed the room and sat down on the bed. Then he lay down, a grin on his face. "This is sure better than the floor. I may sleep around the clock tonight. It not only looks good, but it also feels great."

"I'm glad," Tommie said from the doorway.

Pete sat up. "Why are you standing by the door? Aren't you going to show me the bath?"

"I think you can find your way without my being your guide. I'm going back downstairs to help Teresa."

Pete said, "You're afraid I'll kiss you again, aren't you?"

"Yes, I am. You don't seem to understand when I tell you I don't want you to do that."

"That's not what your lips said to me when I kissed you a few minutes ago." He challenged her with his gaze.

After staring at him, she turned around and went downstairs without a word.

As she reached the first floor, the Williams-Sonoma truck drove up, parking behind the department-store truck. Tommie waited for the man to come to the door and she assured him he had the right place.

She hurried to the kitchen to tell Teresa the delivery had arrived. Teresa ran to the door and guided the movers to the breakfast room with a large, round table, sturdy in build, and six matching chairs.

"Did we order place mats?" Tommie asked as she followed her sister to the kitchen.

"Yes, I unpacked them and put them in a drawer. I'll get them out as soon as I wipe down the table. Oh, I like this table so much."

"You made a good choice."

"Anyone home?" Jim called from the entryway.

Teresa hurried to help him with the food, and Tommie put the place mats out on the new table.

"Wow! It's almost like someone lives here," Jim said. "I like this table and chairs. And the dining room looks good, too."

"Your mother picked it out," Teresa assured him.

"So I've heard."

Teresa looked at him closely. "Didn't she enjoy it? We thought she did."

"Oh, she loved every minute of decorating." Jim managed a smile, but it was clear to both women that he wasn't happy about it.

"Pete's upstairs if you want to check out his bedroom and let him know the food is here," Tommie suggested.

Once Jim had left the kitchen, Tommie turned to her sister. "What did you make of his response?"

"It sounded like his mother had bragged too much about Pete. You know his mother favors Pete."

"I know, but— We'd better set the food out. Did he bring sodas?"

Together the two of them prepared the table.

"If they don't come down soon, I vote we start without them," Tommie said as she popped the tab on one of the sodas and filled a glass.

"I know. I'm starving." Teresa took one of the glasses and put it by her plate with her preference of soda. "Here they come."

The two men joined them and they were soon seated at the table, ready to eat.

"Wait!" Pete said just as they started to eat. He raised his glass. "A toast to the new home, and to the two ladies who've made so much possible."

They all touched their glasses and then got down to the serious business of eating.

* * *

"Thank you for bringing me over to see the dining room, dear. I was eager to see how it looked." Mrs. Schofield walked around the room, a satisfied smile on her face.

"It's lovely, Mom. You did a great job."

"Well, of course, I tried to consider Tommie's taste. After all, when you two… Well, I mean, I know you like her. I told Jim, didn't I, Jim? I told him it will be so nice to see both of you settled down. As soon as your house is finished, I think Jim should get rid of that condo he has. He needs a house, too."

Jim cleared his throat. "Mom, I told you I don't need a house yet. I'll get one when I'm ready."

Pete grinned at his brother. "Not interested in becoming a family man just yet?" he asked as their mother continued her inspection of the house.

"Nope."

"Oh, the kitchen looks lovely, Pete," Evelyn said. "The girls did such a nice job. Have you eaten here yet?"

"We all had lunch together today when Jim brought over some burgers and fries." Pete moved in to the kitchen and opened a cabinet to show his mother the everyday dishes that Tommie and Teresa had chosen.

"Oh, very nice. Now show me the rest of the house."

"They're not finished yet, you know. I told them they only had two weeks, but I've had to put off the party I intended to give because it's taking a while for everyone to get moved down."

"I wondered about that," Jim said. "It seemed to me you were rushing things."

"Yeah. I guess I got carried away. This way, Mom. I want to show you the antique desk Tommie found for me. It's perfect." He led his mother into the study. There was the desk, a leather chair and a credenza.

"I saw some blue wing chairs that would be perfect here in front of your desk. I'll give Tommie a call and let her know where to find them."

"Want to come upstairs and see my bedroom?" Pete asked. "I'm not going to be sleeping on the floor tonight."

"That was so silly of you to do that in the first place. You have a perfectly good bedroom at my house."

"I know, Mom, but I was so excited about the house, I wanted to live here as soon as I could. And it was only for a week. Besides, it's closer to work, too."

"Well, I'm glad you have a bed, instead of camping out here like an uncivilized person."

Jim chuckled behind Pete's back as they all climbed the stairs to the master bedroom.

"Well, this is lovely, but it's a little masculine for my taste," Mrs. Schofield said as she entered the bedroom.

"I requested that it not be frilly."

"What happens when you get married? I mean, you have to make plans for the future."

"Tommie assured me a vase of flowers and some art on the walls will soften the look a little. They were just going for the basics to start with." Pete led her into the bath with its matching blue towels. Then he took her out on the balcony.

"This is so romantic, Pete. You need some chaise longues out here so the two of you can enjoy the summer air."

What was with this woman? Pete thought. Didn't she get that he and Tommie were not a couple? He looked at his brother, a silent cry for help on his lips. But Jim just shrugged his shoulders and said nothing.

Pete knew telling his mother again was not going to help. The woman was as stubborn as a year-old donkey. "I—I'll have to do that, Mom. But later. Much later. The bed is the important thing."

He knew he was in deeper the moment the words left his mouth.

His mother turned a lascivious smile in his direction, then nodded coyly. "Yes, of course, dear."

Beside him, Jim snickered. Pete shot him a dangerous look.

"Mom," he said, "do you want to see the other bedroom furniture?" He had to get her out of his room.

"Of course I do. The girls haven't ordered anything for the living room yet?"

"Not yet. And they still have the family room, too. I want to get a plasma TV in there." He turned to his brother, glad the conversation had gone off in a safer vein. "You can come over and watch baseball games with me, Jim."

"Hey! I have a television."

"But I'm going to buy a big-screen," Pete pointed out.

"Are you going to put in a pool?" Mrs. Schofield asked. "The patio area is lovely, but it would be more attractive with a pool."

Pete shrugged. "I don't know. Not right away. Maybe after I've started a family, it would be a good idea."

"Jim has a club membership. Perhaps you should think about getting one of those. Then the two of you could work out together."

"Right, Mom. I'll think about it."

"Or you could wait until after you're married. Tommie may want something else, or she and Teresa may like the idea of the four of you working out."

"Mom!" Jim protested. "I've told you I'm not dating Teresa."

"Right," Mrs. Schofield said, chuckling. "Next you'll be telling me Pete isn't going to marry Tommie." She walked out the door, leaving her sons staring at each other.

Chapter Nine

"Mom's doing it again!" Jim exclaimed as soon as he was alone with his brother.

"Come on, Jim. It's not like we're teenagers anymore. All we have to do is say no." Pete was enjoying gibing his brother. Call it payback for not coming to his rescue earlier. Truthfully, though, he knew any defense they put up against their mother would be torn down in minutes. Witness his exchange with her in the bedroom, he thought.

"You heard how well it worked tonight, didn't you?" Jim asked, as if reading his mind. He thrust his hands in his pockets and paced the floor in Pete's new office.

"I think you're exaggerating. Mom will probably forget that she thought we were going to marry Tommie and Teresa if you start dating someone else."

"And that's just what I'm going to do. I'm not a satellite to your activities anymore, bro, and I won't marry Teresa just because you're interested in Tommie."

Pete sobered. "I wouldn't want you to. But I hope you're going to be honest with Teresa. I mean, she should know you're not interested in her."

"Don't worry. I'll take care of it." Jim headed toward the door.

"Wait a minute. You're not angry with me, are you?"

"No."

"Then why are you leaving? I thought we were going to hang out."

Jim shook his head. "Not tonight. I'm tired. And I have some thinking to do. I'll catch you later."

Pete followed his brother to the front door and stood there, waiting until Jim was safely in his car.

After he locked up, Pete went to the kitchen for a soda before heading upstairs to his new bedroom. He'd watch the Rangers game and sprawl out on his bed. But after he turned on the small portable TV on the dresser and turned to face the king-size bed, it suddenly appeared way too big…and lonely.

Tommie and Teresa worked hard the rest of the week. Teresa found things for Pete's house that she thought would do. Then she'd take Tommie to look at them in the late afternoons and evenings. Whatever they purchased was scheduled for delivery the next Monday.

There was no sign of Jim and only an occasional

view of Pete. But then, the women weren't at the house in the evenings. Since they had longer before Pete would have his party, they were concentrating on the basics first. Later they would fill in the holes.

"You know," Teresa said on Friday, "maybe I should've become an interior designer. I've enjoyed this work even more than being a kindergarten teacher."

"It's not too late to change," Tommie pointed out. "If you want to take some courses, I'll pay for them."

Teresa hugged her sister. "Tommie, you don't have to pay for classes for me. I've saved my money and even invested some of it. I can pay for the classes, if I decide to take them."

Tommie watched he sister closely. "You seem happy. Is it just because we're doing Pete's house?"

"Well, Jim called. He's taking me out to dinner this evening, just the two of us."

"Oh? And that makes you happy?"

"Yes, it does. He's a…a special person."

"Then I'm happy for you."

Tommie had Saturday off, so she didn't set her alarm. She would get up when she felt like it.

Except that her phone woke her. At eight-thirty, according to her bedside clock.

"Tommie, it's Tab. Have you talked to Teresa this morning?"

"Is something wrong?" she replied in a sleepy voice.

"I don't know. I think so. You know how Teresa is always an early riser. I called her a few minutes ago and she sounded...unsettled."

"About what?"

"That's the thing. She said she wasn't upset, just tired. But...I don't know. She's too sweet to say if someone upset her."

"Did she mention Jim?"

"No. Should she have?"

"She had a date with him last night. Maybe he was still there and she was too embarrassed to say."

"Do they have that kind of relationship?"

"I don't know. I think it was headed that way. I'll call her."

"Okay."

Tommie shoved back the covers and swung her feet to the floor. She headed for the kitchen first and put on some coffee. She didn't want to call Teresa and intrude on her love life, but she and Tabitha knew their sister was too gentle a soul to stand up for herself. They had always taken care of Teresa even when she insisted she could manage on her own.

With a cup of coffee in hand, Tommie dialed Teresa's number.

"Hello?"

"It's Tommie. How are you?"

"Tabitha called you, didn't she?" Teresa demanded.

"Yes, only because she was worried about you. Are you all right?"

"Yes, I'm fine. I had a late morning. There's no law against it."

"How did it go last night?"

"Last night? Oh, you mean Jim."

Tommie heard distress in her sister's voice no matter how much she tried to hide it. "Yes, Jim."

"He wanted to break it to me gently that he wasn't interested."

"Oh, honey, I'm sorry."

"Please, Tommie, I'm a big girl. At least he was honest with me. That's better than being lied to."

"Yes, it is, but—" Tommie held her tongue. Her sister deserved her privacy. "Okay, we were just concerned about you."

"I know. You're my two watchdogs, but there's nothing to worry about."

"How about lunch? Want to go to that tearoom we visited a couple of months ago?"

"Not today. I've got a lot to do, but thanks for the invite. I'll talk to you soon."

"Teresa? You're sure you're all right?"

"I'm fine, Mother Hen. I'm going to have a lazy Saturday. Absolutely no shopping."

"All right. I'll talk to you later."

Tommie hung up the phone. After a minute of staring into space, she got dressed, grabbed her keys and got in her car. She didn't waste any time when she got to Pete's new house. She hurried up the sidewalk and rang the doorbell.

It took several minutes before Pete came running down the stairs, only a pair of jeans on. He carried a T-shirt in his hand but he hadn't managed to get it on yet.

Her mind went blank when he opened the door. All she could do was stare at his broad chest. Again.

Pete spoke first. "Tommie, come in. Uh, was I expecting you?"

"No. But I wanted— That is, I'd like— Do you have any coffee?"

"Sure. Follow me," he said with a smile after closing the front door. He led the way to the kitchen as he pulled on his T-shirt and immediately filled the coffeemaker. "Want some toast? Oh, wait a minute, I have some of those frozen toaster pastries. How about one of those?"

"Yes, that would be fine. I'm sorry, I should've brought something with me. I didn't think—"

"Tommie, are you upset about something?"

"No! Yes. I mean, I am, but it's not your fault."

"But you came to me? I'm glad to hear you trust me."

He retrieved one of the pastries from the toaster and put it on a plate. Then he did the same with the other one and slid one of the plates in front of Tommie. "Have a seat, honey. The coffee will be ready in a minute."

Tommie sat on one of the stools at the breakfast bar. Somehow, things weren't going the way she imagined. After staring at the pastry, she looked up at Pete. "I—"

"Need a fork? I'll get you one. And a napkin, too. You can't say I don't know how to entertain," he added with a smile.

By the time he supplied those items, the light on the coffeemaker had come on. He got out two mugs and poured each of them a cup. "Do you take yours black?"

"Yes, thank you." Tommie grabbed the mug and took a long sip of the coffee. After setting the mug down, she said, "I shouldn't have come."

Pete looked up in surprise. "The coffee is that bad?"

"No, but I made a mistake in coming here. I'm sorry I bothered you."

She got up from the stool and tried to leave, but Pete grabbed her arm and stopped her.

"Eat your breakfast, Tommie. Then we'll talk if you want. If you don't, we'll figure out something else to do. Just relax."

Tommie took a deep breath and sat back down on her stool. His assurance that she didn't have to talk took the pressure off her. She took several bites of the pastry and accompanying sips of coffee before she spoke again.

"I shouldn't have come, but I worry about Teresa and Jim told her last night he didn't intend to see her again. I know it's his choice, but—"

"He told me he intended to make things clear to her. I'm sorry if it hurt her feelings."

"I don't understand why. He never showed any unhappiness or disinterest. Was he pretending?"

"Blame it on our mother."

"Your mother?" Tommie asked in surprise.

Pete stared at his coffee cup before he answered. "When we were seniors in high school, I dated a cheerleader."

Tommie wasn't surprised by that revelation.

"She had a friend who had a crush on Jim, so I asked Jim to double with us. Somehow, it became a habit encouraged by my mother. Before Jim knew it, the girl expected a ring and caused a big stink when he said no."

"Oh."

"It was bad. She didn't keep her unhappiness to herself. She said things and Jim was embarrassed. He didn't date another girl the rest of the year. And he vowed he'd never get caught in that kind of situation again. And Monday night, Mom made a few comments that left Jim unsettled."

"Thank you for telling me that," Tommie said with a sigh. "At least it makes sense now. But Teresa…she's the baby, you know, and kind of naive."

"The baby? What, she's a whole five minutes younger than you."

Tommie's chin came up. "Eight, actually. But she weighed the least, and was always the last to reach certain skills. And she's a kindergarten teacher, for heaven's sake. It's not like she deals with adults all day."

"That's true. She's the nicest person I've ever met."

Tommie straightened and stared at him. "Well, thanks a lot!"

"I didn't say the most interesting person. That would be you, Tommie."

Tommie let her shoulders slump. "I don't see how I could be that interesting. I'm perfectly normal."

"For one thing, you're beautiful," Pete said, leaning toward her.

"No prettier than Tabitha or Teresa. After all, we're identical."

"I think I could tell the difference even if you all wore your hair the same."

"How?" she challenged him.

"Maybe it's because you're determined. You might scare kindergartners, but Teresa never would."

"No, she wouldn't. She's almost as innocent as her students."

"And she has two big sisters who protect her?" Pete asked, raising one eyebrow.

"We try. She keeps her problems to herself these days. We have to press her to find out anything." Tommie frowned at the thought.

"Maybe she's trying to tell you something, Tommie. Teresa's not a child."

Tommie glared at him. "I know that. That's why I shouldn't have come over here."

"I'm always glad to see you, sweetheart. In fact, if you'd given me some notice, I might've made pancakes for you."

"I thought you couldn't cook," Tommie reminded him.

"That doesn't include pancakes. I bet you can cook a few things, too, if you were pressed."

"Of course I can! But not gourmet things, things for company."

"What can you cook? How about meat loaf? I love meat loaf."

"I hate it!"

"I didn't think anyone could hate meat loaf."

"Well, you're wrong."

"But can you cook it?"

"Yes, but so can you. It's not rocket science."

"Hmm. So we'd only have to have a caterer on entertainment occasions, not for every day?"

"We who?" Tommie snarled, daring him to make his remark clear.

Pete took a sip of coffee. "I was just thinking about you and me. After all, you said you couldn't cook. I was envisioning someone who needed instructions to use the toaster."

Tommie got off her stool. "I need to leave. Sorry I bothered you."

"If you'll give me time to shower and change, I'd like you to go shopping with me. Mom said she'd seen some blue chairs that would look good in my office. And I want to look at some art to go on the walls, but I don't trust myself to choose anything."

"I haven't had my shower, either."

"Okay, go home and get ready and I'll pick you up in…let's say forty-five minutes."

She stared at him. Finally, she nodded. "All right."

"You like that?" Tommie asked, her voice rising in disdain. She and Pete had decided to visit a local gallery to find some art for his home.

"Yeah, I do. You don't?"

"It's just globs of color splashed on a canvas. Anyone could do that!"

"But I like its creative energy. We could hang it in my office and pick your kind of paintings for the living room."

She looked away. It wasn't the first time he'd referred to their decisions as part of her future as well as his. She needed to set him straight on that. "Buy it if you want it." She turned and asked the attendant to come help them. In no time, Pete had his energetic modern painting, to be delivered on Monday.

There was a landscape with a field of bluebonnets, the Texas state flower, that Tommie had lingered over earlier, but she'd said nothing about it. After all, they'd already bought one pricey painting.

Pete stopped in front of it. "This is nice. Do you like it?"

Tommie stared at him. Was he teasing her? She cleared her throat. "Yes, I like it, but I think—"

"This artist is famous for her landscapes," the attendant said. "It's quite an investment."

"I think that would look good either in the dining room or the living room." Pete stared at the painting a minute longer. "Hey, it would be great in my blue bedroom, wouldn't it? It would soften the space up, like you said."

"Yes, but an expensive painting in the bedroom wouldn't be seen by many people," Tommie pointed out.

"We'll take it," Pete said, not bothering to argue with her.

"Are you sure, Pete?"

"Yeah, I'm sure. Someone recommended we go to an auction, too, to look for paintings."

"Well, sir," the attendant said softly after looking around. "There's an auction in about two hours near here that's going to have quite a few paintings. None like these two, but you might find several others you like."

Pete asked for directions.

The salesman told him how to find it and suggested they go early to view the paintings before the auction started.

"That sounds like fun. Thanks." Pete caught Tommie's hand and hurried her out of the gallery.

"Pete, I've never been to an auction. I don't know how to— Wait!"

Pete leaned down and kissed her lips, a brief salute that left her confused. "It will be fun, I promise. We'll look at what's to be auctioned. Then, if we see something we like, we'll get a paddle with a number on it. You can hold it up when we want to bid."

"But what if I make a mistake and you end up with something you don't want?"

"That won't happen," he assured her and held open his car door for her to get in.

Tommie gave him an unsettled look, but she got in the car.

When they reached the auction, they found numerous things they liked. There were some beautiful leather sofas for the family room, three paintings, several lamps and a coffee table with matching end tables.

Pete marked them all in the listing so they'd know when the items were coming up for bid.

"That's a lot to buy all at once," Tommie said with a frown.

"More economic this way. I'll have to hire a mover if we buy any of the big things. Better to load up his truck at one time."

"I guess so." Then she saw an old wooden trunk. Something about the object drew her. "Isn't this beautiful?"

"Yes, but what would you do with it?"

"It would make a wonderful coffee table in the family room. Look how well the trunk would go with the leather sofas."

"You're right," Pete said with surprise in his voice. "I wouldn't have thought of that combination, but it would look good."

"I'll have to clean and polish the chest, but you

wouldn't have to worry about propping your feet on it to watch a game or something."

"I'll mark the item on my list," Pete assured her. "You're going to be one busy bidder, honey."

"*I'm* not going to bid. You are."

"Okay. Then you get to hold the list and give me warning."

They settled in the folding chairs set out for the auction and waited for it to begin.

"We make a pretty good team, Tommie. It would be boring if we liked all the same things. This way the house will be more interesting."

"But you may hate to live there."

"No, I'm loving it," he assured her with a warm smile that made her look away.

The auctioneer assumed the podium and smacked his gavel. "Ladies and gentlemen, take your seats, please. We are ready to begin." As he recited the rules for the auction, Tommie listened very carefully. Suddenly she caught Pete's big grin, knowing he was laughing at her, but she raised her chin and remained focused on the auctioneer.

When the man began the auction, Tommie was amazed at how fast it went. She clutched the listing and warned Pete several minutes before anything they were interested in came up for bid.

Like a pro, Pete raised his paddle at the appropriate times.

Tommie was amazed at the low prices for some of the items. And she found the entire process exciting.

As if reading her mind, Pete handed her the paddle. "The next item is that old chest. You bid for it."

After giving him a long look, she took the paddle and waited for the auctioneer to begin the bidding. When it started at fifteen dollars, she readily held up the paddle. Two minutes later, she'd bought the trunk for forty dollars.

"Good job," Pete whispered.

She nodded, but her attention was already fixed on another item they'd looked at. She didn't offer to return the paddle to Pete.

He sat back with a grin and let her do the bidding.

In the end, they bought everything on their list but one painting. Tommie had decided the bidding went too high. It wasn't her most favorite, so she let it go.

Pete went to the cashier with the paddle, paid for their purchases and made arrangements for someone to deliver them. When he came back to Tommie, he put his arms around her. "You did a great job, Madame Decorator." Then he kissed her.

She hurriedly backed out of his arms before she gave in to the urge to stay there. "We—we need to call it a day. It's almost seven o'clock."

"Right. But we're going out to dinner to celebrate our success. Then I'll take you home."

"But you already bought me lunch, Pete."

"You only eat once a day? No wonder you're so slim."

"No, but—"

"Glad to hear it. Let's go. I'm starving."

Chapter Ten

"But why won't you come tomorrow?" Tommie asked Teresa. "I want you to see all I bought."

"I'll drop by during the day, but since you don't need me to be there for the deliveries, there really won't be anything I can do."

"But, Teresa, I'll need help deciding where to put the paintings. You're much better at that than I am."

Teresa paused. Then she said, "I'll come in the morning and stay for a couple of hours, but I don't want to be there if Jim is coming over. It would be too embarrassing."

"You know, Teresa," Tommie said slowly, "Pete explained why Jim reacted the way he did."

"Jim made it clear, Tommie. You don't need to explain. And after a while it won't matter if I see him, but the four of us in the house is too symbolic of what he's faced in the past."

"Okay, if you can come in the morning, then I'll understand when you have to leave."

"Thanks."

Tommie hung up the phone. Teresa sounded better today. Tommie couldn't blame her for refusing to be at the house if Jim came over. She was right. It did sound too much as if Jim was being forced to see her. But Tommie hated that. Part of the fun of doing the work for Pete was sharing it with Teresa.

She didn't even get to share the excitement about the trunk.

She'd have to wait till tomorrow.

Tommie saw Pete only as he was walking out the door Monday morning. Dressed in a tailored blue suit, he explained he had a meeting that couldn't be avoided.

"The coffee's on, ladies," he told Tommie and Teresa. "I'll check with you later." Then he leaned over and kissed Tommie goodbye and headed out the door.

"Friendly, isn't he?" Teresa said with a grin.

She ignored her sister's comment. "Come on, let's go have some coffee. I only had one cup at home." They walked into the breakfast room and kitchen, and Tommie paused to sigh. "This house is beautiful, isn't it?"

"Sure is. Makes me think I need a job where I make more money. I like nice things too much," Teresa said with a smile. Then she held up her hand. "Don't offer to buy me things, Tommie. That's not what I meant."

"I know it wasn't, but I could—"

"No, you couldn't. Part of what I like is finding bargains that make the room look good."

"Oh, I haven't told you about the auction," Tommie said as she got down the mugs and poured the coffee. "Let's sit at the table and— Oh! Here's a box of doughnuts."

"Maybe they're not for us."

"They are," Tommie said, her cheeks red. "He left a note." She crumpled it before her sister could read his sentiments.

"Ah, well, that's nice of him. I could use a little extra sugar this morning."

The two sisters sat at the table and enjoyed their coffee and doughnuts. After Tommie told Teresa about the auction, and in particular the trunk, they discussed family news.

"Mom is dating someone?" Tommie demanded in surprise. "I didn't know that."

"That's because you weren't home yesterday. She called me about four o'clock. She was so nervous."

Even Tommie couldn't hold back a grin at the picture Teresa painted of their mother. Ann Tyler was a beautiful woman in her early fifties and had had the opportunity to date before. But she'd always put her daughters before any man.

"I think that's great. Did she have a good time?"

Teresa grinned in return. "I called her this morning. She tried to sound cool, but I think she did."

"I'm going to call her right now," Tommie said, taking out her cell phone.

Just as her mother answered, the doorbell rang. "I'll get it," Teresa said, expecting it to be a delivery.

When she swung open the door, she discovered Jim on the doorstep.

"Is Pete here?" he asked.

"No, he's in a meeting at the office. Tommie's here if you want to talk to her." She backed away from the door so he could enter without coming close to her.

He frowned but said nothing as he entered.

"In the kitchen," Teresa added. But she didn't follow him. She wandered into Pete's office and sat in the chair behind the desk.

If Jim intended to stay, she'd make up an excuse and leave. She wouldn't be accused of trying to trap him into marriage ever again!

When she heard the front door close a few minutes later, she got up and returned to the kitchen.

"There you are. I wondered where you'd gone," Tommie said as she came back in. "Jim wanted to know if his mother could hang out with us today. She's a little depressed because one of her friends died unexpectedly yesterday."

"Oh, how sad. So she's coming here?"

"Jim thought it would be better than her sitting at home all alone. He's a very good son."

"Yes, he is. I gather he's taken care of her all the years Pete was in Boston."

"Yes. I doubt Pete realizes what a burden that can be."

"Probably not. Did you talk to Mom?"

"Yes. She had a great time. They're going out for dinner this evening. He wanted to go last night, but she thought she shouldn't seem too eager," Tommie said with a laugh.

"That's sweet, isn't it?"

The doorbell rang again. Teresa didn't move.

"I'll get it," Tommie assured her.

This time it was the van from the auction. They began bringing in the furniture. Before they finished, Jim returned with his mother. She immediately became entranced with the new purchases.

Jim stepped up to Tommie's side. "Tell Pete he'll need to take Mom home this afternoon. I'll be in a meeting starting at two and I don't know when it will end."

"Of course. We'll take care of her."

"I really appreciate it," he said to Tommie, but his gaze was on Teresa, who was directing the men. "Everything okay here?" he finally asked.

"Why, yes, everything's fine. Don't worry, Jim, we'll entertain your mother."

"Thanks." He strode down the sidewalk toward his car.

Teresa pretended she didn't even know he'd gone,

but Tommie saw the tension in her shoulders disappear as his car pulled away.

Mrs. Schofield stood quietly as the loaders moved the furniture in. But when the trunk was brought in, she exclaimed, "Oh, that's darling. What are you going to do with it, Tommie?"

"I need to clean it up and polish it, but it's going to be the coffee table in the family room."

"What a marvelous idea. Oh, I'm so glad I came here today. You and Teresa are such good company." Then she started crying.

Tommie put her arm around Mrs. Schofield. Unfortunately, as far as she could see, Pete's grocery shopping had not included tissues. In the kitchen, Teresa dug some out of her purse.

"Come sit down on one of the new sofas, Mrs. Schofield. They're very comfy," Teresa said, leading her there.

"Oh my, yes." She sniffled between each word. "They're lovely. Just perfect for watching television."

"Yes. Unfortunately, Pete hasn't bought one yet," Tommie told her.

But Pete's mother needed to talk about her friend. Teresa and Tommie sat beside her and let her tell them about the woman who'd meant so much to her. They supplied the tissues and listened. After a while Mrs. Schofield ran out of words, but they sat quietly.

Finally, she looked up at them. "You girls are so wonderful. When I try to tell Pete or Jim a problem, they think they have to fix it. All I needed was someone to listen."

"That's why we have friends. Your friend sounds like a wonderful woman." Tommie hugged her again. Then she got up. "Now, we need to figure out where to hang our paintings. Did you see all of them?"

"I saw two," Evelyn said, "and I liked them very much. Are there others?"

"Oh, yes, we bought two others at a gallery. I forgot they hadn't come. One is a field of bluebonnets, and the other is a modern painting that Pete wanted for his office. Oh, and we bought the two blue chairs you recommended for his office."

They discussed the placement of the sofas in the family room and whether the lamps should go in the living room or family room.

Suddenly Mrs. Schofield said, "I'm hungry!"

Tommie checked her watch. "Well, no wonder. It's after one o'clock. Would you like to go to a restaurant?"

"Couldn't we get takeout? I look terrible after all that crying."

"Mrs. Schofield, you look fine, but takeout works for me," Teresa agreed.

"Call me Evelyn. It would make me feel younger."

"Evelyn, it is," Tommie agreed. "I'll run and get some food. How's Chinese?"

"Oh, I love it."

"I'll only be a few minutes," Tommie promised after

she took down their preferences. Then she hurried away, leaving Teresa with the task of entertaining Evelyn.

But the phone rang almost at once. Teresa answered. "Schofield residence."

"Hi, it's Jim. I wanted to check on Mom before I went into my meeting. Is she doing okay?"

"She's fine. Here, I'll let you talk to her." She handed the phone to Evelyn.

The conversation went on for a few minutes, with Evelyn praising her and Tommie. Teresa mentally shrugged her shoulders. She couldn't be mean to Evelyn just to satisfy Jim.

After Evelyn hung up the phone, she turned to Teresa. "I am so lucky that my sons are interested in such nice girls."

Teresa sighed. "Jim's not interested in me, Evelyn. In fact, I'm not even sure Pete is interested in Tommie. We're working for him, that's all."

Before Evelyn could answer, Tommie came back with the food, much to Teresa's relief.

After they ate their lunch, the gallery paintings arrived, and shortly thereafter, the blue chairs. Arranging all the furniture kept the women busy till five o'clock.

"I don't know where Jim is," Evelyn said, looking at her watch. "He should be here by now."

"He had a late meeting. I know Pete was going to take you, but we can run you home," Tommie assured her.

"You've put up with me all afternoon. You shouldn't

have to drive me home, too. I can just wait for Pete. Doesn't he usually come home at five?"

"We don't really know, Evelyn," Tommie said.

"Well, let's call his office." Evelyn grabbed the phone before either woman could protest. She dialed the number from memory and soon had Pete on the phone. "Dear, I need you to come drive me home. I don't want the girls to go out of their way."

"Where are you, Mom?"

"I'm at your house. I came over today because I was upset about Lilah's passing. You remember? I told you yesterday."

"Oh, yeah. Uh, is Tommie there?"

"Of course she is. What girls did you think I was referring to?"

"Yeah, let me talk to Tommie."

Evelyn handed the phone to Tommie. "He wants to talk to you."

"Hello?"

"I'm sorry you've been stuck with Mom all day. I didn't know she was coming over."

"Jim brought her over."

"Is she still upset?"

Tommie looked at Evelyn, obviously listening to the conversation from her end. "No, we've had a lovely day. Wait until you see your office."

"She can hear you, right?"

"Yes."

"I've got about half an hour more work I have to

do. Then I'll come take all of you out to dinner. I'll call Jim—"

"No! Uh, he's in a meeting."

"Okay, just the four of us. You three decide where you want to go."

"Pete, you don't have to buy our supper. You and your mother can—"

"No arguments." He hung up the phone before she could say anything else.

"Pete says he'll be here in half an hour. He insists on taking the three of us to dinner." Tommie looked at her sister, hoping she realized Jim would not be included.

"What about Jim?" Evelyn asked.

"He's tied up in a meeting, remember?" Teresa said.

"Oh, that's right. Well, too bad for him. We'll just be missing one of our family. Now, where shall we go?"

Family? Now Tommie knew where Pete got his stubborn streak and tunnel vision.

As Evelyn babbled on about restaurant choices, Tommie exchanged an exasperated look with her sister. They were trapped!

Pete loved his home office, and the dinner went well, except for Evelyn's occasional remarks about loving a "family evening."

Then she asked if the girls would be at the house tomorrow.

Pete preempted their reply. "Maybe I could get away and take you to lunch, Mom."

"Well, that would be nice, dear," Evelyn said, "but the girls are such better listeners."

Tommie had to stifle a laugh at the comment and the look on Pete's face. She kicked Teresa under the table, and her sister shared the smile.

But Teresa, as always, saved the day. "Maybe tomorrow would be a good time to set up a luncheon with Mom. You said you wanted to meet her," she reminded Evelyn. "I could go with the two of you. There's a nice tearoom we've gone to before. Would you like that?"

"Oh, that would be lovely. I'm dying to meet your mother. She's done such a wonderful job raising you girls."

"Let me know the time and I'll try to join you," Tommie said.

Teresa nodded. "I'll call you both in the morning."

When they left the restaurant, Pete took hold of Tommie's arm and held her back. "Thanks for making the day easier for Mom. I didn't even realize—"

"I know. But Jim did."

"Yeah, I've got to get better about picking up the slack. But you and Teresa did a great job today. I owe you."

"No, you don't. Your mother is a delightful woman. We enjoyed her company."

She tried to pull her arm from his hold, but he didn't let go. Instead, he aimed for her lips. She put her hand up. "No, you're not supposed to do that. I work for you, remember?"

"Yeah, I remember. But a kiss of gratitude shouldn't be ruled out. And I'm *really* grateful."

"Pete—"

He kissed her, as he always did now when they parted. When had that become his custom? Tommie couldn't remember exactly. She only knew she liked it. Way too much.

Tommie got to the tearoom shortly after Teresa. Their mother and Evelyn had been seated.

"Sorry I'm late," she said as she slipped into one of the chairs.

"Hi, Tommie," Evelyn immediately said. "I'm so glad you made it. I just met your mother."

Ann Tyler smiled at her daughter. In her early fifties, she was still slender and there were only hints of gray mixing with her blond hair. "I haven't seen much of you lately, Tommie."

"I'm sorry, Mom. I've been busy with Mr. Schofield's company move. And then he hired Teresa and me to furnish his new house."

"So I've heard," her mother said.

Evelyn suggested they show Ann the house after lunch.

"I'd love to see it," Ann assured her. "I never got to do much decorating, but I love looking through the magazines."

Despite their opposite backgrounds, her mother and Evelyn looked as if they'd hit it off, Tommie realized. They found they had a lot in common, particularly the experience of multiple births. Throughout the tea and on the ride to Pete's, she and Teresa had little to do to carry the conversation.

After she let the group in to Pete's, she told them she had to get back to work. She hurried out before she could give in to Teresa's panicked look at being left alone with the two mothers. She crossed her fingers and hoped that everything would go well.

When she got home that evening, Tommie found her answering machine blinking with four messages. She pressed the button and poured herself a glass of iced tea while she listened.

The first call was from Teresa. "We survived the afternoon and I think Evelyn and Mom really enjoyed it. I'll talk to you later."

Message number two was from her mother. "Darling, I really liked Evelyn. But she seems to think there's more between you and Pete besides decorating his house. Is that true?"

Tommie made a mental note to call her sister and find out what Evelyn had said. But it couldn't have been too bad since Teresa hadn't mentioned it earlier.

The next message was from Evelyn, raving about her afternoon and offering thanks to Tommie and Teresa for having invited her.

Okay. That was good. And she didn't mention anything about her sons.

Number four was Pete. "Honey, just wanted to see how the luncheon went today. Jim wanted me to tell you how grateful he was, too. How about dinner? I don't feel like cooking and I thought we could grab something together. Call me."

She clenched her teeth and fought the urge to immediately pick up the phone to call him. She absolutely mustn't give in to the inviting warmth in his voice. Absolutely.

So why was she reaching for the phone?

Chapter Eleven

When Tommie said she had no preference over a restaurant, Pete suggested one known for its down-home cooking where the men frequently went for lunch.

Tommie admitted to herself they could've gone to the North Pole and it wouldn't have mattered to her. Which frightened her.

When they reached the restaurant, they found a crowd waiting to be seated.

"I guess we caught their dinner rush," Pete said with a grimace.

"It doesn't matter. I'm not that hungry…yet." She gave him a teasing look and he instinctively drew closer to her.

"Pete! Hey, I didn't know you were coming here,"

Bill called. He was standing with Adele at the front of the line. "Come on up here. We'll just ask for a larger table."

"Okay, great," Pete said. Then under his breath, he muttered, "Sorry." Slipping his arm around her waist, he moved the two of them forward.

"Hi, Adele, I didn't know you were back," Tommie said with a smile.

The hostess was ready to seat them, so Adele called over their two children who were playing a video game nearby. "We decided to come on down after they loaded up our furniture. Bill's taking a couple of days off to help me entertain the kids. Thanks for your suggestions on places to take them."

"I'm sure they'll love it here."

"I'm hoping that Robbie will be in your sister's class," Adele said as the kids came over. She introduced Robbie, five, and his sister, Diana, who was seven.

"There are only two kindergarten classes," Tommie explained, "so you've got a fifty-fifty chance. But I'm sure Robbie will do fine with either teacher."

Adele nodded. "Diana's going into second grade, but she's more worried about what she should wear. Back in Boston we'd be buying sweaters, but I'm not sure about Texas fashion."

Tommie had no idea what kids wore these days.

"Why don't you ask Teresa to talk to Adele?" Pete suggested. "She might even be willing to take them shopping."

"I'll talk to her," Tommie said. "But she may not have time." She ignored the question in Pete's eyes.

The waitress came to take their order then, and afterward Pete suddenly said, "Say, I need to ask you kids a question. Your dad says he cooks a lot. Do you like his food?"

"His spaghetti is good," Robbie said enthusiastically.

"That's because we get Rocky Road ice cream afterward," Diana added.

Pete grinned at Bill. "Oh, I see."

Bill defended himself. "Hey, I told you I make good spaghetti. I never said I was a pastry chef."

Adele leaned over and kissed his cheek. "And I'm grateful for that spaghetti once a week."

"I'm sure," Tommie said. "I couldn't imagine you could come home every night after a demanding job like yours and face cooking dinner every night." A sales representative for a major cosmetics firm, Adele had managed to get a transfer to Dallas. "I'd probably eat out half the time."

"That's better than me," Pete volunteered. "I eat out almost every night."

"Even with that beautiful kitchen Bill told me about?" Adele asked.

Tommie hadn't realized Bill had seen Pete's place. "You've been to the house?" she asked.

"Yeah, I went by one day during lunch. Pete wanted to show me his office."

"Well," Tommie said to reassure Adele, "your house has a warm and efficient kitchen, too. Have the kids seen the new place?"

"We're waiting until we close on Thursday," Adele replied.

"Mom says my room has a window seat," Diana said.

Adele leaned over to Tommie. "I want to tell you something. I dreaded this move. I didn't want to leave Boston. But you've made everything so easy for us. I can't thank you enough."

Her cheeks becoming hot and red, Tommie tried to dismiss the compliment, but Pete heard it and put his arm around her. He raised his iced tea in a toast. "To Tommie."

Everyone joined in, even the kids. But they cheered even louder when Pete said, "And after dinner, there's ice cream—my treat."

After they left Bill and Adele at the ice-cream parlor and were driving home, Pete asked, "What's up with Teresa?"

Tommie stared straight ahead as she figured out what to say. "Nothing."

"Then why did you hesitate when I suggested Teresa might take Adele and her daughter shopping?"

"Why wouldn't I hesitate? I can't commit Teresa to do something without checking with her. She's not on your payroll, you know. I mean she is for the furnishing of your house, but taking people shopping isn't what we agreed to."

Pete said nothing for a couple of minutes and Tommie hoped he would drop the subject. She should've known better.

"So how much do I have to pay to get Teresa to go shopping with them?" There was a hardness in his voice that she'd never heard before.

"I didn't mean Teresa would ask for money, though there's no reason why she shouldn't. Her time is as valuable as anyone else's. But I can't promise she'll do something."

He stopped in front of Tommie's condo. "Will you at least ask her? Tell her I'll pay for her time."

"Money isn't the answer to everything, Pete," Tommie retorted, hating his response.

"It's worked with you, hasn't it? In fact, I'd say it's the only thing that's worked with you. Everything you've done for me and my people is because you're being paid, right?"

"Do you charge for your expertise? I don't see you giving away your software, or whatever you create. You've got a lot of money and it must've come from somewhere. All I'm trying to do is earn a living!"

"A living? Or a fortune?" he said with a sneer.

Tommie couldn't take any more. She opened the door and got out of the car. "Save your money, Pete. Teresa and I don't want it. Nor do we want to help you with your house or your people. Find someone else to do your work for you. Maybe someone who'll do it for free."

With that, she slammed the door and hurried into her condo.

Pete wandered the spacious rooms of his home. What had gotten into him? Of course Tommie was working for him and should be paid. Why had he acted that crazy?

Each time he asked himself that question, he found another aspect to consider…because he didn't want to face the answer.

He'd been attracted to Tommie from the start. But he hadn't considered her a good choice for his wife. He treated the position of wife as he would any other position. Tommie's résumé didn't include cooking or entertaining. She didn't want to stay home and raise their children while he conquered the world. She had a successful career and ambition. She seemed interested in money.

And he wanted her to do everything for love.

In fact, he wanted a woman a great deal like himself to completely change and be something she wasn't.

That idea struck him like a gale-force wind. Tommie's attitude couldn't be right, could it? It was man's place to earn the money and woman's to take care of the home. Wasn't it?

He went to his home office and settled in the chair behind the desk and called his brother.

"Jim?"

"Yeah? You still up?"

Pete looked at his watch. It was midnight on a work-day. Jim must've been asleep. "I'm sorry I called so late, but...I need to talk something out."

"And it can't wait?" Jim asked.

"No. I may have already messed things up."

"Okay, why don't you come over and I'll put on a pot of coffee."

Pete got back in the car. He found an all-night gro-cery on the way and bought some brownies from the in-store bakery. He had to offer something to his brother for letting him interrupt his night's sleep.

Soon they were both sitting at the table in Jim's breakfast area, eating brownies and drinking coffee. Pete didn't say anything at first. Suddenly he wasn't sure he wanted to hear his brother's opinion. He did, but then again, he didn't.

"So, what's going on?" Jim asked in a casual voice.

Just hearing Jim's calm response helped settle Pete's nerves.

"It's Tommie."

"I figured."

"How did you know?"

Jim gave him a wry grin. "I've seen you in love be-fore, but not with a woman like Tommie. There were bound to be problems."

"Yeah."

"Is it that you have different tastes? Has she deco-rated the house in a style you hate?"

"No, not at all. She's got great taste. You've seen what she and Teresa have done."

"True. And it certainly can't be that she isn't pretty enough."

"No, of course not!"

"Could it be because she isn't a meek little woman, willing to stay home and raise a lot of kids? Does she intend to continue to work and expect any husband to split the chores with her? Is that the problem?"

"You're laughing at me!" Pete protested with a glare.

Jim grinned and picked up another brownie. "These sure are good," he commented before he took a bite.

"Aren't you going to help me?"

"I'm not sure I can. You have to decide what you want in a wife. And she has to decide what she wants in a husband."

"What about chemistry?" Pete suddenly asked. "Isn't that important?"

"Oh, yeah."

"Well, Tommie and I have chemistry. I feel like I know her better than anyone. I could tell her apart from her sisters blindfolded."

"So, what's the question? You want her to be with you. What are you willing to sacrifice for that happy ending?"

Pete got up and began to pace. "I don't see why I have to sacrifice anything!"

"Really? As Dr. Phil would say, how's that working for you?"

Pete fell into his chair. "Not well."

"So, what do you have to do?"

"I guess I have to change what I want. Do I negotiate with Tommie? Interview her like she's applying for a job?"

"I wouldn't, if I were you."

"No, I guess not. She's not even speaking to me right now."

"Why not?"

"I accused her of only doing things for money."

Jim frowned. "Are you giving away your software now?"

"That's what she said, too."

"What brought on your accusation?" Jim asked, studying his brother.

"Adele was worried about how to dress her little girl. I suggested Tommie ask Teresa to talk to Adele or go shopping with them. She wouldn't commit to that idea."

"Because she had to talk to Teresa first," Jim said, sounding incredibly reasonable.

"I decided she was playing me for more money," Pete said, nearly wincing as he did so.

"What? You didn't!"

He felt himself get a tad defensive. "I did. It could be true."

"What was her response?"

Pete turned away from his brother. "She told me to

keep the money I agreed to pay them for the decorating, because she and Teresa were through."

Jim just shook his head and took another bite of brownie.

"I know it was stupid," Pete continued. "Now I have to apologize to her, but I think I need to know what I want before I do that."

"Have you slept with her?"

"No. She even protests when I kiss her."

Jim frowned. "Then she's not interested."

"She kisses me back. Her words tell me to stop, but her lips tell me she's interested."

"Have you discussed any of this with her? Does she want to continue working?"

"Yeah. And she says she not only can't cook, but doesn't want to either."

"Do you?"

"Well, I can make pancakes, but that's about it."

"So maybe you learn how to make a few things and you can split the chore."

"What about when we have kids?"

"Hire a housekeeper. You'll do that anyway while you're alone in that big house. I can't see you cleaning the bathrooms and vacuuming the carpet."

"No, me neither. Do you have a housekeeper?"

"I have a maid service that comes by once a week. But as big as your house is, you'll probably need someone two days a week right now."

"Damn, I should've asked Tommie about that."

"You're kind of helpless, aren't you?" Jim said with a teasing grin.

"Watch it, brother, or I'll start a food fight."

"Not in my kitchen," Jim said firmly. "We'll go to your house for that kind of mischief."

Pete stood and offered his hand to his brother. "Thanks for helping me think things through. I guess I'll be groveling tomorrow."

"Good luck. I think Tommie's not going to forgive you anytime soon."

Pete shook his head. "Don't I know it."

The next morning after she got to work, Tommie arranged for a pick-up by a local delivery service. She had prepared a listing of her and Teresa's costs and had stapled all the receipts to the list. She didn't take gas money or the payment Pete had promised. In the envelope she included the checkbook he'd given her so that everything would be back in his hands.

There would be no need to see him again.

Then she remembered she had a key to his house. She quickly pulled out her key ring and removed that one. Slipping it into the envelope, she then sealed it and gave it to her secretary to hold until the service picked it up. Then she went into her office and closed the door behind her.

Dialing her phone, she waited patiently until Teresa answered.

"Hi, how are you doing today?" she asked Teresa brightly.

"Fine," Teresa said, sounding normal.

"I need to ask a favor of you. We had dinner last night with Bill and Adele. She was asking what little girls wear to school here. I promised I'd ask you."

"Sure. I can make a list for her, or if she wants company on a shopping trip, I'd enjoy that."

"Are you sure?" Tommie asked. "Adele would love that, but I know you've got a lot to do."

"Not all that much. Unless there's something imminent for Pete's house."

Tommie sank her teeth into her bottom lip. "Mmm, actually, we're not going to do any more work on his house. I've got the money he owes you. Shall I transfer it to your bank account?"

There was a pause, as if Teresa was thinking about what she'd said. Then she only used one word. "Why?"

"It doesn't matter, Teresa. It's not anything you did. He and I clashed and I didn't want to continue to work with him. He's a big boy. He can take care of his own house."

"That's true, but I enjoyed the shopping. He was willing to pay us the full amount?"

"Yes, he was. He realizes how much work we did," Tommie said hurriedly.

Teresa sighed. "You're lying, Tommie. You know I can always tell."

"Look, it's my fault you're not getting the money, Teresa, so it's only fair that I pay you."

"Absolutely not! I won't take it, Tommie. Decorating Pete's house was a pleasant experience for both of us for a while, but I think we're better off without the Schofields, with their hang-ups and their money."

"You're sure you're all right with that, Teresa? I feel bad that I promised you—"

Teresa interrupted her. "Don't be silly. I had fun. But I'm going to try something new for the rest of the summer."

"What?"

"For years I've had an idea for a children's book, and I'm going to try writing it this summer."

"That's wonderful!" Tommie exclaimed. "You'll do a great job."

"Thanks for your enthusiasm, sis. I can always count on you."

"We can always count on each other, Teresa. You, me and Tabitha."

After she said goodbye to Teresa, she checked her schedule for closings. Then she went through the new listings that had come out. There were several she wanted to see on the Realtor tour.

When her phone rang, she called to her secretary to answer it and take a message. Somehow, she had a feeling it would be Pete.

She was right. He apparently argued with her secretary, but the woman held firm.

After that, Tommie called the hotel where Adele and her children were staying.

"Adele? It's Tommie. Teresa said she'd be glad to go shopping with you and your kids, if you still want to."

"Oh, yes! I was talking to one of the other mothers this morning. We're all obsessing over the same thing. How many can come?"

"I—I suppose as many as want to."

"Oh, thanks, Tommie. I'll tell Pete—"

"That's my only request, Adele. Don't tell Pete."

"Why not?"

"I'm not working for him any longer. Our going shopping isn't part of a service we're providing. It's something fun we want to do."

"Oh, Tommie, you and Teresa are so generous with your time. I won't tell Pete if you don't want me to, but he should know what a nice person you are."

"No, thanks, Adele. He already knows more than he wants to know."

But she had no intention of letting him know how badly he'd hurt her last night.

Chapter Twelve

Pete was frustrated. All day he'd tried to reach Tommie, both on her office phone and her cell. Obviously she wasn't taking his calls.

Finally he called Adele at the hotel. "Have you talked to Tommie today?" he asked.

Adele paused. Then she said, "Yes, I did."

"When was that?"

"This morning."

"What did she say?"

"She said that she was no longer working for you."

Pete sighed. "That's true, for the moment."

Adele remained silent.

Finally Pete said, "I'll find someone to help you go shopping for the kids' school clothes, Adele. It can't be that hard."

"That's all right, Pete. I know you're busy. The wives have all been talking and we're going to go shopping together. We'll talk to the salesclerks. We'll be all right."

"You're a trouper, Adele. If you talk to Tommie again, tell her...tell her I need to talk to her."

"Sure. Did you try her office?"

"Yes. Thanks, Adele." Pete hung up the phone. He'd even considered going to Tommie's office, but he knew she'd simply refuse to see him.

He probably needed to give her more time, but first he needed to apologize. But how, if she wouldn't talk to him? Then he thought of a way. *Say it with flowers.* He remembered the ad slogan. He picked up the phone and ordered roses to be delivered to her before the end of the workday.

He dictated an apology that he hoped would sway her opinion of him—and prayed the teenager taking the message could spell.

He debated parking outside her condo, but she would probably just accuse him of stalking. No, all he could do was wait.

Pete snickered to himself. He could design software, manage millions, hire and fire. But waiting was not his forte.

A dozen red roses got delivered to Tommie's office just as she was preparing to leave work. Her suspicions about the sender were confirmed when she read the card attached.

Please forgive me. I'd like a chance to explain my
sudden stupidity.

Pete

"I bet you would," she muttered to herself. She
started to crumple up the paper, then stopped. Instead,
she carefully put it in her top desk drawer, facedown.
She didn't want to read his words every time she opened
the drawer, but she did need a reminder not to get per-
sonally involved with her clients ever again.

"Ooh, beautiful flowers. You got a steady beau, Tommie?" one of her co-workers asked as she passed Tommie's office on her way out.

"No. Just a jerk who owed me an apology. Nothing
personal."

"Well, he certainly apologizes nicely."

Yes, he did. But it didn't matter. She'd known from
the first that she wasn't what he wanted. He was the one
who persisted, persuaded, extended their relationship
long past its natural expiration date.

She felt a twinge of pain when she thought about his
house. It had been her favorite house on the market. To
have the chance to furnish it had been great fun. It was
hard to give up the mental possession she'd begun to feel.

"You're a fool," she said to herself. After all, she'd
known it would never be her house. She'd known its
owner would never marry her. She wasn't a happy-
housewife type.

Her office phone rang as she was gathering her things

to leave. By instinct she picked it up. As Adele answered, she realized it could've been Pete. She'd have to be more careful.

"How are you doing, Adele?"

After exchanging pleasantries, Adele explained that she was calling on behalf of some of the relocated wives who had middle-school and high-school-aged kids. "Will Teresa know what those students wear?" she asked.

"I could ask Tabitha," Tommie replied. "Maybe she'd know."

"That would be great. Apparently the kids are stressing about fitting in at school."

Tommie could relate. "I can remember how I felt as a teenager. Those are difficult years."

"I can't thank you enough. The mothers will be thrilled."

After they hung up and Tommie made some notes to herself, she once again picked up her briefcase and headed for the door. But her departure was blocked for the third time that night. This time by Pete, whose appearance brought her to an abrupt halt.

"Good. You're still here," he said, stopping a few feet from her.

She said nothing.

"Did you get the roses?"

"Yes." She wanted to back away, but she was determined not to let him see how much he upset her.

"Have you forgiven me?"

"There's nothing to forgive, Mr. Schofield. As you

so clearly pointed out, all there is between us is business. Now that we've severed our business ties, there's nothing."

"Tommie, you know better than that," he protested and stepped closer to her.

"No, I don't. Now, if you'll excuse me, I have an appointment." She tried to move around him.

At first, she didn't think he would move and let her pass. He hesitated, but then he stepped back, disappointment on his face.

"We're not finished, Tommie, and you know it."

She hurried for the elevator, his words following her.

Pete called several times throughout the week, but Tommie left standard orders with her secretary. She was always out to Pete Schofield. But Friday she took the day off for the shopping spree. Tabitha had agreed to go with the older group after they all met at Hulen Mall.

Tommie gave them a brief rundown of the normal Texas weather for September through November. Definitely not winter. Even December through February wasn't horribly cold, except for one or two brief cold snaps.

Then they split up. Since Teresa had the larger number of mothers and children, Tommie stayed with her. Teresa talked to the salesclerks, explaining the situation and the needs of the group, and the clerks immediately took over. Teresa only put in a word when the kids went to the overly expensive stuff.

At the end of the day, Tommie told Adele what else she'd done to help the kids fit in. "I talked to several soccer coaches last night. Do any of the kids besides yours play sports?"

"Yes, a couple of the boys do. You mean we could get the kids involved in some programs this summer?" Adele asked, her eyes lighting up.

Tommie nodded. "And I've checked the neighborhood for kids who might be in their classes. I thought I could contact the parents and see if we could arrange a get-together so your kids could have some friends before school starts."

Reaching out to touch Tommie's arm, Adele was almost in tears. "Tommie, I can't tell you what that would mean to them. And if our kids are happy, we're happy."

"And that's my goal."

Adele hugged her. "Now, we've made plans to say thank-you to you and your sisters. Our husbands are waiting for all of us at a nearby restaurant so we can buy you dinner."

"That's not necessary," Teresa said quickly.

"Yes, it is. Please don't say no. We've tried to think of ways to thank you, but we couldn't come up with anything else."

Tommie and Teresa exchanged glances. Tommie knew why she didn't want to join them, and she was pretty sure why Teresa didn't either. They were afraid Pete or Jim would be there. But it would be rude to refuse.

"Is Tabitha coming, too?" Teresa asked.

"She's certainly being invited," Adele assured her.

When they arrived at the restaurant, they discovered it had a back room that they had reserved. Tommie took a quick look around and didn't see Pete. She drew a relieved breath, only to have him walk up behind her.

"Nice job, ladies. I owe you a debt of gratitude," he said, obviously speaking to the three sisters.

Tommie said nothing, stepping behind Teresa.

"We were happy to help. These are such nice people," Teresa said.

Tabitha appeared more relaxed. "What are you doing here, Pete? You don't have any children...that I know of."

"Nope, I don't, but I hope to one day."

Adele suggested they all sit down. Tommie tried to make sure she wasn't sitting with Pete, but he grabbed the chair next to her.

Fortunately, he didn't try to talk to her until after their meals were ordered. Tommie enjoyed the respite. But she knew he wouldn't waste his opportunity. He was too much like her to do that.

"Have you forgiven me yet?" he asked under his breath without looking her way.

"No." She turned to talk to Tabitha, who was seated on her other side.

He waited until she was silent again.

"I said those things because I wanted you to do everything because you loved me."

"Of course. That's an excellent reason to insult me."

"I didn't say my behavior was rational. A man doesn't fall in love willingly."

The pain around her heart eased slightly, but she fought any relenting on her part. "I don't believe anyone asked you to fall in love, willingly or unwillingly." She continued to face forward, refusing to look at him.

"Didn't you?"

That question brought her face around so she could glare at him. "I beg your pardon?" Her voice contained absolute outrage.

"You certainly didn't attempt to minimize your sexual attraction," he murmured with a grin.

"You're enjoying this, aren't you?" she demanded.

"At least you're talking to me. You've refused my calls all week."

"I was busy."

"No one is that busy, and you know it."

She refused to respond.

"Honey, I goofed up, and I know it. But how can I make it up to you if you won't even see me?"

"You apologized nicely with the roses." She was again staring straight forward. Looking at him weakened her determination.

He softly whispered, "I've missed you."

"I'm not what you want, remember?"

"I've changed my mind. As Jim says, I've moved into the twenty-first century."

"I—I don't believe you."

Pete took her hand and brought it to his lips. "Sweetheart, I started off wrong. I thought I could make a list of what I wanted in a wife and I'd find someone who fit my requirements."

"You made that quite clear," she said stiffly.

"But I was wrong! That's what I'm trying to tell you. I fought my feelings for you because you didn't fit my list."

"You don't have to keep telling me that! I'm not trying to trap you, Mr. Peter Schofield. All I want is for you to leave me alone!"

As if she couldn't bear their conversation any longer, Tommie jumped up from her chair and ran from the room. The conversation died and everyone stared at Pete.

"Uh, excuse us," he muttered and followed Tommie out of the room.

He found her in the hall that led to the restrooms. She was leaning against the wall, tears running down her cheeks.

Her eyes were closed, but he figured she knew he'd come after her. "Tommie," he said softly as he clasped her shoulders.

Her eyes opened. "Go away and leave me alone!"

"Is that really what you want?"

"How dare you ask me that question!"

Having recognized his mistake, Pete acted instead. He pulled Tommie into his arms and covered her lips with his. He kissed her with all the pent-up feelings that had festered in him the past week.

"Oh, Tommie, I've missed you so much," he murmured.

Tommie felt herself leaning into him, giving in to Pete's persuasions. She tried to stop, to push away, but his strong arms held her in place.

She turned her head away, freeing her lips. "Pete Schofield, stop kissing me right now!"

"Why?"

"Why?" He needed to ask? "Because you said I'm not right for you!"

She thought she'd made herself clear, but he moved toward her lips again. "Didn't you hear me?" she asked, sidestepping him.

"Yes, but I was wrong. That's what I'm trying to tell you."

"I haven't changed, Pete! I don't even want to be a gourmet cook."

"I don't want to be, either."

"Nor do I want to stay home and clean toilets!" she yelled.

"Me neither."

"I—I don't like modern art!"

"That's okay with me."

In her frustration, Tommie reached out and smacked him on his chest. "Stop it!"

"Stop what?"

"Agreeing with me. We don't want the same thing!"

"You want to know what I want, sweetheart?"

Her tears began coming fast and furious now. "No, because you don't want me!"

"That's where you're wrong. I found out that the *only* thing I want, the *only* thing I need, desperately, is you."

"No, you want the perfect housewife. That's what you said. And that's not me!"

"I love you, Tommie, just the way you are. Nothing would make me happier than for you to marry me." His lips found hers again, and this time she could not resist. She gave herself over to the kiss.

"I won't apologize for what I am," she warned him when they broke off the kiss.

"I wouldn't want you to, honey. I want you just the way you are."

Tommie stared at him, still a bit skeptical. "Are you sure?"

He nodded.

"But—"

He put a finger to her lips. "No buts allowed."

"How do you know you won't change your mind in six months?" She needed to be sure. She couldn't give her heart and have it broken. Not to this man.

"Because I can't imagine life without you, whether it's six months or sixty years."

"You understand I'm a career woman?"

"Just like I'm a career man."

"And if we have children?"

"We'll find a way to deal with it. I promise."

It was true, then. He did love her. Her heart leaped with joy and she threw her arms around his neck. "Pete, I love you so much!"

"Then why were you crying when I was trying to explain to you?"

"Because it sounded like you were arguing with me."

Pete gave a rueful smile. "I guess I need to improve my communication skills. We can practice all you want. Especially after our wedding."

Bringing her lips a hairsbreadth from his, Tommie said with a smile, "We could have a Christmas wedding."

Pete, who had started to kiss her, abruptly halted. "Christmas? Uh, Tommie, could we negotiate the date? Christmas is a long way off."

"But weddings take a long time to—"

Now he kissed her deeply, his mouth cutting off her words, his arms holding her close against him.

"We could be ready by October," she said.

He kissed her again, and this time he must have pulled out all the stops, because she could barely breathe.

Then he whispered, "Couldn't we make it a little sooner? I think it might get difficult to wait that long."

"Hmm, let me think," Tommie said slowly. "Kiss me one more time."

She lost track of the number of kisses he gave her. But by the time Tabitha came out to discover them in the hallway, wrapped in each other's arms, nothing had been decided.

"Hi, guys. Everyone is looking for you."

"We're fine. In fact, we're more than fine." He looked at Tommie. "Sweetheart, may we tell them?"

"Yes, Pete. That way you can't back out of it," she said, a teasing look on her beautiful face.

Pete didn't hesitate. He wrapped an arm around her and led her back into the private dining room. "Ladies and gentlemen, allow me to introduce my future wife, Tommie Tyler."

The room broke into applause.

Pete led Tommie around the room so everyone could congratulate them. Tommie was beaming until Tabitha and Teresa surrounded her. "We're so happy for you, sis," Tabitha said. "Have you told Mom?"

"No. I didn't know myself until just now."

"Well, I don't want to be a worrywart," Teresa added, "but Evelyn is going to expect to be told right away."

Tommie took a deep breath. "You're right. But maybe Evelyn will think she already knew, since she's been teasing Pete about our marriage ever since she went shopping with us."

"At least you know she'll be happy for you. And Mom, too," Teresa said with a smile.

"And both of you are happy, too?"

"Of course we are," Tabitha assured her.

Teresa squeezed her tightly to her. "We just want you to be happy."

"Oh, I am," Tommie said, beaming at her sisters. "So very happy!"

Epilogue

Once both mothers had been informed, they happily, of course, took over planning the wedding, including setting the date.

"It's not like we're dependent upon our families to make decisions for us, Tommie," Pete said.

"That's true, but we're not eloping, either. It takes time to plan a wedding."

Pete wrapped his arms around her. "Do you realize how little time we'll have together until after the wedding?"

"Will we? I mean, I know weddings can take a lot of time, but—"

"But we could rush it, work fast, and then have a honeymoon. Doesn't that sound better?" He kissed her.

"Mmm, yes, but I'm not sure we could do it."

"You've got two sisters on vacation. They'll help you."

"I know they would, but…well, Tabitha has been so busy, and Teresa hasn't been feeling well lately."

"Honey, you worry too much about your sisters. Ask them if they'll help you. With your organizational skills, we could be married in a week!"

It took three weeks rather than one, but on July 10, they were married in a small wedding that had grown big. All the corporate families that had moved to Texas with Pete were there, as well as Pete's and Tommie's friends. Tabitha and Teresa were the bridesmaids and Jim and Bill were the groomsmen.

Evelyn cried all during the ceremony. Not because she was upset with the marriage, but because she was so happy. Ann was overjoyed, too. Her friend, Joel, offered to give Tommie away. Since Tommie suspected he would soon be a part of their family, she gladly agreed.

"That was a beautiful wedding, Mrs. Schofield," Pete whispered in Tommie's ear as they danced to a beautiful love song.

"Thank you, dear sir. But I think you know me well enough to call me by my first name."

"I know, but I like calling you Mrs. Schofield." He kissed her before swinging her around the dance floor. "When can we leave?"

"We haven't even cut the cakes yet, Pete. And that chocolate cake looks good enough to die for."

"I have something more exciting in mind." He whispered his plans in her ear.

Tommie's cheeks turned bright red. "I'll try to speed things up," she promised and slipped away. Pete moved off the dance floor, keeping his gaze on Tommie.

"You afraid she's going to get away?" Jim asked, grinning at his brother.

"Not if I keep an eye on her," Pete replied with a smile.

"She's not going anywhere, bro. She's as crazy about you as you are about her."

"Damn, I hope so!"

Jim laughed at his brother's intensity.

Pete, his gaze still on his wife, jumped when she waved to him. "She wants me to join her." He hurried across the room.

"Mom says we can cut the cakes now. I told her we had to catch our plane and didn't want to be late."

"You're wonderful," he said, grinning.

She slid her arms around his neck. "So are you, but I get a piece of the groom's cake before we go. Okay?"

He kissed her. "For you, my love, anything.

* * * * *

Be sure to look for the next
LONE STAR BRIDES *title*
THE TEXAN'S TINY DILEMMA
(Silhouette Romance #1782)
by Judy Christenberry.
On sale September 2005

If you enjoyed what you just read,
then we've got an offer you can't resist!

Take 2 bestselling love stories FREE!

Plus get a FREE surprise gift!

COMING NEXT MONTH

#1782 THE TEXAN'S TINY DILEMMA—
Judy Christenberry
Lone Star Brides
Theresa Tyler's hidden pregnancy wouldn't prove half as difficult as interpreting the father's response. Sure, she burned for James Schofield, but she wanted to be chosen by *his* heart, not by his upright nature. Were his actions only dutiful gestures, or did something lurk beneath them? If only she could trust what *her* heart was telling her, and not her head!

#1783 PRINCE BABY—Susan Meier
Bryant Baby Bonanza
Marrying Seth Bryant only two weeks after meeting him was Princess Lucy Santos's most spontaneous moment. But when Lucy learned she was pregnant with Seth's son—her country's future king—she found herself caught up in a web of royal desires and private concerns. Would these threats blind the young couple to their original desires—or would love reign triumphant?

#1784 THE SHERIFF WINS A WIFE—Jill Limber
Blossom County Fair
When Jennifer Williams left Blossom County for the lure of big city life, Trace McCabe was crushed by the knowledge that he'd never see the love-of-his-life again. But eight years later, Jenn was back in Blossom—temporarily—to help her pregnant sister, and Trace vowed to do whatever it took to win the heart of his first love….

#1785 ONCE UPON A KING—Holly Jacobs
Perry Square: The Royal Invasion!
Three months ago Cara Phillips shared a night with a gorgeous mystery man only to find him gone when she awoke. Imagine her surprise when she shows up to serve as bridesmaid at a wedding and learns he's not only her friend's brother but a prince to boot! But will the prince ride off into the sunset once he learns Cara's most closely guarded secret—or can this fairy tale have a happy ending after all?